W.i.t.c.h.

Will   Irma   Taranee   Cornelia   Hay Lin

Trust Your Heart

Adapted by ALICE ALFONSI

HYPERION PAPERBACKS FOR CHILDREN
New York

© 2007 Disney Enterprises, Inc.

W.I.T.C.H. Will Irma Taranee Cornelia Hay Lin is a trademark of Disney Enterprises, Inc. Hyperion Paperbacks for Children is an imprint of Disney Children's Book Group, L.L.C.

Printed in the United States of America
First Edition
1 3 5 7 9 10 8 6 4 2

This book is set in 12/16.5 Hiroshige Book.
ISBN-13: 978-1-4231-0288-5
ISBN-10: 1-4231-0288-6
Visit www.clubwitch.com

ONE

BRRRINNNGG! BRRRINNNGG!

The moment Will Vandom walked into her house, she knew something was wrong. The phone was ringing, but her mom was making no move to answer it. She sat like a marble statue, her arms stiffly folded, her gaze fixed on thin air.

"You're home early," Will called.

That was strange, too. Her mom had a high-pressure job at Simultech. She hardly ever came home from work early. Yet there she was, parked on the living room couch, still in her business clothes.

"What happened?" Will asked. "Did they fire you?"

"No jokes, Will," her mother snapped.

1

"It's been a very rough day."

BRRRINNNGG! BRRRINNNGG!

The phone continued to ring. Will frowned. Whether it was her mom's boyfriend, Mr. Collins, or one of her coworkers at Simultech, someone must have made her angry. Her mom usually leaped to get incoming calls. It was rare that she wouldn't want to talk to anyone.

BRRRINNNGG! BRRRINNNGG!

Exasperated, Will moved to answer the phone herself.

Suddenly her mom sprang off the sofa and grabbed the receiver. "Hello?" she said. "Hello? Who's there?" Will couldn't help noticing that her mother's pretty face looked stressed, even a little fearful. Mrs. Vandom pushed back her long, dark hair, listened intently, and then— *Bang!*

She slammed the receiver down so hard it shook the small wooden end table. "Get lost, and stay lost!" she shouted at the phone.

Will groaned. *Just what we needed,* she thought, *another prank call to cheer things up!*

Over the past week, they'd gotten half a dozen strange calls like that one.

It's a pain, Will thought, *but it's not exactly*

the end of the world. Considering what I'm going through with Matt, and the events I've lived through as a Guardian, there are a lot *worse* things than getting a few prank calls.

"Everything's fine," Will's mom insisted before Will could even ask. "Food's ready in the kitchen. Let's go eat."

Will dropped her backpack and shrugged out of her jacket. "Actually, I'm not very hungry today. . . ." Not after seeing Matt at school, she added silently.

Sorry, she wanted to tell her mom, *but when the guy you love prefers another girl, it's enough to kill your appetite for a decade!*

BRRRINNNGG! BRRRINNNGG!

Not *again,* Will thought.

"I'll get it," her mom announced sharply.

"Don't bother—" Will began, but her mother was already moving toward the end table again.

"Don't you think I know who this is, you idiot?" Will's mother cried into the phone. "If you don't cut it out, I'll make your life miserable! But your life must already be pretty pathetic if you've got time to waste on these stupid phone calls!"

Will couldn't believe her mom was losing it like that. Somebody had probably just copied the wrong number into his speed dial or something, she thought. Why couldn't her mom just chill?

After her mom finished shouting into the phone, she got very quiet. For once, the crank caller actually seemed to be saying something. Will's mom listened for a few seconds. Then she blushed, pulled the receiver away from her ear, and covered the mouthpiece.

"It's for you, Will," she said quietly. "It's your swimming coach."

Will stared at her mom in horror. "Whaaaat?" Mr. Deplersun was the toughest swim coach she'd ever had, and her mom had just called him an *idiot*!

Will's mom held out the receiver sheepishly.

Will snatched it from her. "You could at least have apologized!"

"Would you do it for me?" her mom asked.

Will closed her eyes and pressed the phone to her ear. "I'm sorry, sir," she said, totally embarrassed. "My mother thought you were, uh . . . somebody else."

"That's good to know," the coach replied in

his gruff voice. "I figured she didn't like me."

"Oh, no, sir—" Will began, but the coach cut her off.

"I'm calling because I just finished checking your freestyle times," he said. "You're officially being called to the trials for the next meet. I want you in the pool in half an hour!"

"Okay, I'll be there," Will said calmly, but inside she was shouting, *Yessss!* After she hung up, she let it all out. "Yes! Yes! Yes! Yes! I did it!" She jumped up and down all over the room, showing little regard for the furniture.

Her mom put her hands on her hips. "Down from the couch, young lady!"

Will bounced off the cushions and onto the floor. She threw her arms around her mother's neck. "For a special occasion, could we cut a deal about my being grounded?"

"What special occasion?" her mother asked. "What are you talking about?"

"Something that's really important to me," Will said. She hoped her mother would let her off the hook so she could go and train. After all, getting grounded in the first place wasn't even her fault—not entirely, anyway.

The previous week, without a word, Will

had apparently left their apartment in the dead of night . . . only, it hadn't been *Will*. The girl who'd run away had been *Astral Will*, her magical double.

Will, along with her friends Irma, Taranee, Cornelia, and Hay Lin, were Guardians of the Veil and were often called on to protect the universe from evil. When that happened, they would change into their Guardian forms and create astral-drop replicas of themselves to take their places at home while they traveled worlds away.

During their last adventure, Astral Will was supposed to have been living Will's life in Heatherfield while the real Will was off fighting to keep Candracar safe from an evil ex-Guardian named Nerissa. After returning home, she was *supposed* to reunite with her double, and in so doing absorb all of the astral drop's experiences. Everything Astral Will had seen, heard, felt, or thought would become part of Will's memories.

That was what was *supposed* to happen. But it didn't. Astral Will had gone MIA. Why? Because during Will's time away, Astral Will had seen something extremely upsetting: it was Matt Olsen embracing a pretty, dark-haired girl.

Matt Olsen was the boy Will had given her heart to. For more than a year she'd waited for him to hold her, kiss her, and tell her that he loved her . . . but he still hadn't. And, thanks to her drop, at last she knew why. He was in love with someone else.

The affection between Matt and this unknown girl had been unmistakable. Their embrace had been real and close. And when she finally got to see the moment through her drop's memories, it had made Will finally realize that she'd been a complete fool.

Astral Will hadn't taken it well, either. The night she saw Matt embracing the dark-haired girl, she had completely freaked. Hurt, confused, and afraid, she had stolen Will's photos of Matt from her desk drawer and run away.

With the help of her four friends and fellow Guardians, Will had finally tracked Astral Will down. They had brought her back home, where Will had been able to reunite with her double. The damage, however, had already been done. In more ways than one.

When Will's mother discovered her daughter missing in the middle of the night, she'd called the police to search for her. And *that* was why Will had been grounded when she got back from saving Candracar and the rest of the universe.

Will wasn't happy about being put under house arrest, but she couldn't very well blame her mother. It wasn't as if she could just blurt out the truth ("Excuse me, Mom, but I have this magical double, and *she's* the one who ran away, not *me!*").

Actually, the last person who'd run away like that on her mom had been Will's father. Back when they'd lived in Fadden Hills, he'd left them without even saying good-bye. Her mom had gone through a terrible time, and Will was sorry she'd put her through anything even close to that again.

When she and her mom had first moved to Heatherfield, they fought all the time. Lately, though, they'd been working to improve their strained relationship. They had just been starting to get along, and then Astral Will had to go and ruin it!

Nice reward for fighting unscrupulous evil head-on, huh? Will thought. But then, nobody had ever promised the Guardians balloons and ice cream for doing their job. Being a Guardian had as many challenges as it had benefits.

There were times when Will wanted to tell her mother everything that had *really* happened to her since they'd come to Heatherfield. As Keeper of the Heart, however, Will was also keeper of Candracar's secrets.

Candracar was a dimension that was everywhere and nowhere. It was the place where an ancient, ethereal being, known as the Oracle, watched over the entire universe. The Oracle was also Will's cosmic boss. He was the one who'd anointed Will and her friends as Guardians of the worlds he watched over, including Earth.

Each of Will's friends was gifted with power over an element. Irma was able to move water, shift waves, and divert raindrops. Taranee could create and manipulate fire. Cornelia was able to command earth, rocks, and plants. And Hay Lin had the ability to control air.

Alone, none of their powers were very effective. When the girls came together, however, as W.I.T.C.H.—a name they'd formed using their first initials—they were an awesome force. As their leader, Will was able to unite and magnify all of their abilities with the help of the ancient crystal amulet she carried inside her.

The Heart of Candracar, as the amulet was called, was sometimes a burden, but Will had been born to guard it. No matter how difficult being the Keeper of the Heart became, Will knew that the Heart was her responsibility and her destiny. Whenever Will was called upon to unite the Guardians to fight evil, she felt its ancient magic pulsing through her. The Heart transformed her from an average middle-school girl into a winged being of fantastic power. The experience, however, was far from an everyday one. Most of the time, Will simply lived her life the same way she always had before becoming a part of W.I.T.C.H.

Swimming, for instance, was something she'd been serious about for years. Slicing through the water, Will felt powerful and sleek. In a way, swimming provided an escape for her.

In Fadden Hills, when her parents started to fight all the time, swimming had made Will feel as though she were in another world. Propelling herself in an almost weightless state through the pool, she had felt far away from all their yelling and door-slamming.

After she became a part of W.I.T.C.H., Will

had understood the reason that swimming had always felt so special. It was the only activity she'd ever experienced that came close to Guardian magic.

After the coach's phone call, Will tried to explain some of this to her mother—not the Guardian part, but the part about how important swimming was to her. She explained how she'd qualified for that evening's trials. And she pleaded with her mom to suspend her punishment so she could try out for the next citywide meet.

Her mom listened to Will's case. She thought about it for a minute. And then she agreed to let her go!

"Yes!" Will cried. Once again, she jumped up and down in the living room—this time avoiding the couch. She ran to the kitchen to grab a protein bar. That was all she had time to eat if she were going to make it to the city pool on time.

"Good afternoon, Miss Will!"

The cultured voice echoed in Will's head as soon as she entered the kitchen. The voice didn't come from a butler, however, but from the refrigerator.

In addition to their main powers, all of the Guardians had an array of quirky talents. Will, for instance, was able to converse with animals and—weirdly enough—appliances.

"You were granted permission to attend your swimming practice, Miss Will," the fridge, said. "Aren't you pleased?"

"I guess so, James," Will told the fridge, whose name was James, "but I don't understand why Mom gets so bent out of shape over those stupid prank calls."

Will noticed a dozen long-stemmed red roses in the trash. She bent down and saw that they were still wrapped up in tissue paper and ribbons.

"Hey, Ed," Will said to the phone on the counter. "She didn't have a fight with Mr. Collins, did she?"

"From what I know, the happy little love-birds are getting along just fine," Ed, the phone, replied. "As for the roses, they came this morning, with no note."

Will's brow wrinkled. Hmmm, she thought. If Mr. Collins didn't send these, then who did? Mr. Collins is the only guy Mom's been dating . . . that I know of, at least.

"Ahem . . . greater discretion would be appropriate, Edward," the fridge warned the phone.

Will's hands went to her hips, and she turned toward the phone. "Yes, Edward, and, with discretion, could you please tell me *who's* making those prank calls?"

"My professional ethics keep me from disclosing such information," the phone replied with a proud sniff.

James rumbled. "What Edward means to say is that the phone calls are from an unidentified number, Miss."

"You're such a pain!" the phone snapped. "I hope you short-circuit!"

Will stifled a laugh. "Okay, guys!" she told them, holding up her hands. "Don't get overheated. We'll talk about this later on. Right now, I've got to scoot!"

TWO

Will bounded off the downtown bus and hurried along the sidewalk. Dusk was descending on Heatherfield. Streetlights were flickering on, and the city pool building glowed brightly in the rays of the sunset.

I can hardly wait to get into my suit and slice through that water! Will thought, her excitement growing.

The pool building was dome shaped, and the outside was lined with large windows. Will peered through the glass at the Olympic-size pool, shimmering beneath hundreds of lights. Around it, bleachers that could hold a thousand spectators climbed up toward the high, curved ceiling.

Will quickened her pace toward the front entrance. When she heard a familiar voice, however, she stopped dead in her tracks.

"You'll see," the voice said. "Will's special."

No, Will thought. It can't be him! It can't!

But it was.

Matt Olsen's tall, lanky form stood right in front of the building's double doors. Will cursed her own pulse for racing at the sight of him.

How dare he look so cool and carefree in his floppy bucket hat and loose red chinos? she thought. He *should* be losing sleep. He *should* be as wrecked and frazzled as I've been! After all, *he* is the one who was hugging someone else—not me.

On the contrary, Matt didn't appear distressed in the least. He looked calm and cool standing beside his white motor scooter. And he smiled with relaxed confidence at the pretty girl beside him.

Will took a closer look at the girl and noticed her long dark hair. It's her! she realized. It's the girl my astral drop saw hugging Matt! This was the first time Will had seen them together in real life.

"There she is!" Matt told the girl, pointing

directly at Will. Then he waved his hand in the air like an excited five-year-old. "Will! Will!"

Oh, for crying out loud, Will thought. He's got his girlfriend with him now. What could he want with me? Will glanced at her watch.

Great, she thought, the coach was expecting me five minutes ago! There's no time to find another way in. I'm going to have to deal with them!

Will continued her journey across the crowded sidewalk. The closer she got to Matt, the tenser her body became. She suddenly felt extremely awkward and self-conscious. She knew her short, shaggy red hair was a wind-blown mop, and her old, bulky jacket made her look like a blue marshmallow. But she hadn't expected to run into Matt and his girlfriend at the city pool!

It was hard to look at Matt now. All of the memories her astral drop had held were now fresh in her own mind. And the last person she wanted to see was him. Her fingers tightened so intensely around her backpack strap that her knuckles turned white.

Why couldn't my astral drop have kept her memories to herself! Will silently groaned.

She wished that her memories of Matt were like computer files that got corrupted. Will wanted to delete them all from her mind. She wanted to erase the first night she'd ever seen him, singing with Cobalt Blue at the school Halloween party. She wanted to delete the day they'd first met, when he'd helped her rescue her little dormouse.

She wanted to forget everything else, too. How they'd laughed together, working at his grandfather's pet shop, and how they'd enjoyed each other's company on what she had *thought* were dates.

Now she knew better. They hadn't been dates at all. Matt had just been hanging out with her, like any other good buddy.

Will's mind jumped back to the time Matt had taken her to that fancy French restaurant. Dressed up in their very best clothes, they'd followed the maitre d' into the elegant dining room. When they'd sat down at the table and opened the menu, however, Matt had cleared his throat and confessed that he'd forgotten his wallet.

"These things happen," Will had said at the time.

They'd gotten up and left. It had been totally embarrassing. Matt had said he'd wanted to treat her, but instead, she'd taken Matt to the Golden Diner and bought them both burgers.

During summer vacation, at Irma's family beach house, Will had spilled the details about her so-called fancy date with Matt. Her girl-friends had laughed, and she'd become angry, thinking they didn't understand. Now, however, Will knew the truth.

I was the one who didn't understand, she thought. I was the one who deluded myself into thinking that Matt liked me romantically. But boys don't forget their wallets on *real* dates. Even back then, Matt must have thought of me as just another pal. That's why it was no big deal to him that he didn't treat me when he had said he would.

Will gritted her teeth as another memory surfaced. The Sheffield Institute had been plan-ning a retirement party for Mrs. Rudolph. Most students figured the math teacher had just had enough of teaching. But Will and the other Guardians knew that she was really returning to her home world of Meridian.

On the evening of the party, Will had

approached Matt in the Sheffield courtyard. The night had been chilly but clear, with stars shining as bright as diamonds in the sky.

Will had wandered close to the gym entrance, where torchlight was flickering on the stone pathways and kids were laughing and talking in the shadowy dark. When Will spotted Matt, she did something she'd never done before. She'd run across the grass and thrown herself against him. She'd clung to his lean form, her hands clutching at his faded yellow jacket.

I love you, Matt, she'd thought then, gazing into his liquid brown eyes. Please tell me the same thing. Please!

"You're unique," he'd said instead. "You're unpredictable . . . surprising. . . ."

Tell me that you love me, she'd thought once more. Tell me! Will had held her breath, waiting for him to say it.

"I'd say the right word is . . . indispensable!" he'd finally said.

Matt hadn't said the words Will had been desperate to hear. But even if he had, it wouldn't have mattered. Will soon found out that Matt wasn't really Matt. Nerissa was controlling him!

The words he spoke were Nerissa's. The evil sorceress was only trying to get the Heart of Candracar away from Will. But now Nerissa was gone, and she could no longer interfere.

Will sighed; now there seemed to be an even bigger obstacle in their relationship.

"Here you are. Finally!" Matt called to Will, interrupting her thoughts. "I've been trying to reach you since this morning."

Will approached the happy couple.

"This is Mandy," Matt said, gesturing to the girl. "She's a really good friend of mine."

Duh, Will thought. Gritting her teeth again, she took her first close look at Mandy. The girl was tall, almost as tall as Matt. She made Will feel like a total shrimp. She was shapely, too, with sleek, long, raven hair, big blue eyes, and a perfect smile. In her hand was Matt's extra scooter helmet. It was the very same helmet Matt used to let Will wear!

"Hi!" Mandy said brightly.

"Right," Will replied, her mind racing. Matt and Mandy, Mandy and Matt, M + M, she thought in disgust. How long have they been together? she wondered. How could I have been so blind?

Memories from the week before suddenly flooded her mind. She saw the cell phone in Astral Will's hand, saw Astral Will dialing call after call to Matt. She saw her astral double leaving their apartment building to look for the boy she loved. And then she'd found him, his strong arms wrapped tightly around—

Matt began to say something, but Will had no intention of sticking around to listen. "Sorry," she said, "but I'm in a hurry. I've got trials to—"

"That's exactly why we're here," Matt said. He gestured to Mandy again. "She's here for the trials, too. I thought you could stick together and give each other a hand."

What? Will thought. Somebody wake me up from this nightmare!

"I'm pretty good at freestyle," Mandy bubbled. "How about you?"

I think I'm going to throw up, Will thought. Clenching her fists, she glared at Matt. *Why? Why rub salt into the wound you've already made?* she silently raged. Now you expect me to be her friend? This is crazy!

"Will! Mandy!" a deep voice shouted.

Will turned to see a tall, broad-shouldered

man with short black hair and a goatee. It was Mr. Deplersun, her swimming coach. He stood at the entrance to the indoor pool, wearing a blue tracksuit and an impatient scowl.

"Hi, Mr. Deplersun!" Mandy called to him.

"Um . . . er . . . hello, sir," Will said weakly.

The coach looked at the girls with narrowed eyes. "I didn't call you over here to have teatime with your boyfriend!" he barked. "Get into that pool on the double!"

"Right away, sir," Will promised.

The coach turned from the door and marched back inside.

Mandy shrugged. "Well, bye, Matt . . ." She waved and moved toward the glass double doors.

Matt smiled at Will. Their eyes met, and Will sighed heavily. *He's totally clueless about how much he's hurting me*, she realized. *He figures we're just "friends," so it's totally fine for him to introduce me to his girlfriend. Well, it's not fine!*

Without a word or a wave, Will turned abruptly from Matt and began to walk away. She didn't get more than a few steps before she heard Matt start up his scooter and grumble, "Man, what did I do?"

Will stopped, then turned around. Stomping right up to him, she pointed a finger in his face. "Number one," she shouted, "if you and Miss I'm-Pretty-Good-at-Freestyle came here to make me look bad in front of the coach, you'd have been better off staying home!"

Matt's brown eyes widened. Then he blinked at Will in complete confusion. "I'm sorry, Will," he said awkwardly. "I didn't mean—"

"Number two!" Will continued. "You've got no right to decide what I should do or who I should hang out with. Got it?"

Matt's face fell. He appeared to be stunned, but Will knew what he was probably going to say. So she said it for him.

"I know! I know!" Will cried. "I don't have the right to decide who you hang out with, either, right? So, fine! Just keep on seeing your little Miss Charisma, but don't force me to spend time with her!"

She turned her back on Matt.

Walk away! she ordered herself. Just walk away! But she couldn't. A part of her was desperate for some sort of response. So she folded her arms and waited.

After a few moments of silence, Will glanced over her shoulder. Say you're *sorry*, she thought. Or say you hate me! I don't care, but say *something*!

Matt simply sat on his scooter with a look of complete and utter confusion on his face. Their eyes met. Will waited a few moments longer for Matt to explain himself. Once again, he remained silent, his eyes sad.

"That's it!" Will exclaimed, throwing up her hands. "You aren't even trying to defend yourself. But you know what, Matt? Silence is for *cowards*—the kind of guy I hate most of all!"

Boys! Will thought bitterly as she strode toward the doors to the pool. Who knew they could be so *stressful*?

THREE

Boys! Hay Lin thought happily. Who knew they could be so *wonderful?*

Laughing, she dropped her big purple messenger bag on her bedroom floor. She shrugged off her coat and stepped out of her shoes.

Behind Hay Lin, Tarance did the same. Then she flipped on Hay Lin's small TV and turned the channel to TNN, the news station.

Both girls stepped around the chaos spread out on Hay Lin's bedroom floor. Scattered all over the carpet were art supplies, books laid open, and half-finished drawings.

As the air Guardian, Hay Lin had a creative nature. She could blow through a room starting a dozen different projects in one evening. And that was just fine with her! Artistic types were messy, Hay Lin had concluded long ago, and that was that!

Flopping onto her bed, she peeled off her bright yellow goggles. She used them as a head-band—another example of her kooky, artistic style—but she was tired of wearing them just then. She threw them across the room, where they landed on her cluttered desktop with a *plop!*

One floor below, Hay Lin's parents were preparing the Silver Dragon restaurant for the evening rush. The dining room was still practically empty, although Fang, the cook, already had his kitchen staff bustling. Smells of ginger, garlic, and sizzling sesame oil wafted up, filling the second-floor apartment with appetizing smells.

Hay Lin's stomach let out a growl, and she groaned. She couldn't eat yet. In two hours, she and Taranee were supposed to meet Eric and Nigel at the Rock and Roll Café. Together the four of them were going to write a news article about the café for the school paper. They were each planning to order a few dishes from the menu. Then they planned to share and sample them.

I need to save my appetite for later if I am

going to advise my classmates about what's good or bad on the menu, Hay Lin told herself. She forced herself to ignore her growling stomach, along with the delicious smells drifting up from Fang's woks.

Tossing back her long blue-black pigtails, she glanced at her bedside alarm clock. She could hardly wait the two hours till she would see Eric Lyndon again!

Eric, Eric, Eric, Hay Lin chanted to herself in a singsong voice. *He is the absolute coolest boy at Sheffield!*

Hay Lin didn't bother saying those words aloud, because she knew she'd get an argument. Taranee thought the exact same thing about Nigel, *her* boyfriend!

Boyfriend, Hay Lin silently repeated to herself. It was strange to think of herself as finally having one. For a long time, Cornelia and Will had been the ones with boyfriends. And Irma and Taranee had been into crushin' on boys before Hay Lin.

She had used to think boys were totally gross and completely useless. If they weren't chewing with their mouths open at lunch, they were either playing with bugs, or cackling like monkeys. In her view, boys were either cruel, like Uriah, who bullied half the school, or clueless, like Martin Tubbs, who followed Irma around, panting like a lovesick puppy.

These are my choices? Hay Lin had once thought. Not very appealing.

Then she'd met Eric, although "crashed into" would probably be a more accurate description!

The summer before, she'd been trying to eat an ice-cream cone while wobbling down the street on her Rollerblades, when Eric's motorbike had whizzed by. He had swerved to avoid hitting her, but the long strap of her shoulder bag had gotten hooked on the back of his bike. She'd squealed as he pulled her along, and he had quickly screeched to a stop.

Hay Lin still remembered the reassuring strength of Eric's grip as he helped her up, not to mention the supercuteness of his smile!

Later that evening, he'd totally surprised her by showing up at the Silver Dragon restaurant, looking beyond adorable with his thick, wavy, dark hair and intelligent brown eyes. He'd asked Hay Lin out to watch the meteor shower with him.

It was that night, under the beautiful stars, that she had started to learn all about him.

Eric was new to town, and really smart. He'd traveled all over the world with his parents. Now he was living in Heatherfield and studying with his grandfather, a professor of astronomy.

After that amazing night watching shooting stars, Hay Lin and Eric had become almost inseparable. And even after all this time, she still really liked him.

So tonight, she wanted to look great for him—grown-up, cool, and glamorous. The only problem was . . .

She ran her tongue over the metal on her teeth. Glamorous girls don't wear braces, she told herself. They wear foundation and lip liner!

For weeks, Hay Lin had fought with her mother about getting that mouth full of metal. Part of her had been worried about Eric's reaction. So far, however, he'd been really cool about the braces. In fact, everyone had. Not one jerk at school had called Hay Lin Zipper Lips or Tinsel Teeth, and she hoped they never would. She'd even created her own unique design for the braces, using the symbols for the elements of W.I.T.C.H.! Because of that, she was usually proud to display them.

Unfortunately, when she thought about where she was going that night, she felt unsure of herself. The Rock and Roll Café was a place where older kids hung out. It was totally cool, and Hay Lin worried about whether or not she looked as though she fit in. She thought of all the older girls who would be there and of Eric's possibly looking at them instead of her.

Ugh! she wailed to herself. I wish I hadn't thought of that!

Of course, Taranee already had. She pointed at the glamorous anchorwoman on TV. "There! You see? If we looked like that, we'd be perfect!"

Hay Lin regarded the woman on television with a dubious look on her face.

"Since we're on assignment for the school newspaper," Taranee went on, "we need to be professional about it. We need to look like real reporters and blend in with the crowd."

Hay Lin had a feeling that Taranee was concerned not just with looking like a professional reporter, but with becoming a more sophisticated version of herself so that Nigel would notice.

Hay Lin knew there was a much easier way to look older and amazing. She had mentioned it to Taranee on their walk home, and they had both giggled at the idea of transforming themselves. When they changed into their Guardian selves, the girls were dazzling beings. Their limbs became longer, while their bodies and faces grew mature and more beautiful.

Their outfits were stylish, too—short skirts, purple-and-turquoise tights, and belly-baring tops. If they were to show up at the Rock and Roll Café as the Guardians, all eyes would *definitely* bc on them!

The notion was very tempting, but both girls had quickly rejected the idea. For one thing, it was totally against Guardian rules to transform without a valid reason. Irma had done that once already, and she still regretted it.

Thinking back on that disaster, Hay Lin couldn't help smiling. It had happened after they'd first become Guardians, when they were still getting used to their powers. Irma was crushin' on an older boy, and she had decided to do something about it. Without telling her friends, she transformed herself into the water Guardian.

She hid her wings under a pretty shawl and waltzed right into a hot Heatherfield dance club, looking stunning. The plan worked. The boy she'd been crushin' on totally noticed Irma in her Guardian form. He offered her a ride home, and she happily took it.

When the boy got her alone in his car, however, things got intense. He tried to kiss Irma! Normally, that would have made her happy, but the guy was a creep about it. So Irma became flustered and transformed him into a toad!

Hay Lin still remembered the hours that W.I.T.C.H. had spent in the swamps of Heatherfield, searching for the boy in order to change him back. They'd never gotten so many mosquito bites in their lives!

Taranee had also reminded Hay Lin of another reason they shouldn't transform to impress a boy—Cornelia. When Cornelia had first met her now ex-boyfriend, Caleb, in his world of Metamoor, she'd been in her Guardian form. That was how he'd fallen in love with her. But when he saw her in her regular form, as a middle-school Heatherfield girl, he freaked and broke up with her.

That little reminder finally convinced Hay Lin to drop the transformation idea completely. "Let's leave magic out of it for sure," she told Taranee, jumping back into the present.

Taranee agreed, but she wasn't ready to drop yet another idea for making them look older and sophisticated. She'd bought some items at the drugstore. Now she dumped them out of her bag onto Hay Lin's bed.

Wow! Hay Lin thought. There's so much! She counted five lipsticks, three eyeliners, two mascaras, four different blushers, a bottle of liquid foundation, and tons of face powder. "Are you sure?" she asked, gulping at the sight.

Taranee nodded enthusiastically. "Yes! If we looked like that—" She pointed at the image on the small TV on Hay Lin's dresser—"we'd have nothing to worry about!"

Hay Lin glanced at the screen. The glamorous TNN anchorwoman was delivering the weather. "The storm clouds darkening our skies won't be leaving us for a while," she warned, "but then a gleam of sunshine will be back to make you smile." The woman grinned, practically blinding the viewer with her perfectly straight, white teeth.

"If you want to be a reporter, you've got to *look* like one," Taranee insisted, gesturing to the screen once more.

Hay Lin studied the TNN reporter's look more closely. Beneath the perfectly plucked brows, she wore three different colors of eye shadow and loads of mascara. Her cheeks were smoothed with foundation and dusted with pressed powder. Her dazzlingly bright smile was framed in equally bright lipstick. And her carrot-colored hair was piled on her head in a high-fashion bouffant.

Hay Lin wasn't so sure she'd look good in orange hair—or that much makeup. She frowned at the array of cosmetics on her bed.

"I'm not convinced, you know," she told Taranee.

"You don't want to wear makeup?" Taranee asked in a disappointed tone.

"I didn't say that," Hay Lin replied. "I'm just saying that we're really putting on makeup because tonight we're going out with Nigel and Eric . . . and not because of the article."

"Er . . . well . . ." Taranee mumbled.

"Well," Hay Lin said with a shrug, "let's just hope our new reporter look helps us out on both fronts!"

Taranee laughed. "Now, hold still."

"Just make sure the colors match my braces, okay?" Hay Lin teased with a giggle.

A few pounds of cosmetics later, Taranee finished working on Hay Lin. She passed Hay Lin a hand mirror.

"Turning to the latest fashion news," the TNN anchorwoman announced on TV as Hay Lin took in her face, "it looks like this year's hot new look is a cross between sweetly aggressive and frighteningly beautiful!"

Well, I've got the frightening part down, Hay Lin thought in horror. "Are you crazy!" she screeched, gazing at her reflection. Her delicate ivory complexion had disappeared under layers of makeup base and pressed powder. Garish lipstick had turned her mouth into a ridiculous Valentine's Day heart. Bright circles of blusher turned her cheeks redder than a circus clown's, and the line of her dark, almond-shaped eyes was totally ruined by a thick rainbow of eye shadows.

It was *not* a good look.

Taranee shrugged. "If at first you don't succeed, try, try again."

"Oh, no, you don't!" Hay Lin cried. "It's *my* turn to put it on."

I must have been crazy to let Taranee do my makeup! Hay Lin thought as she ran to the bathroom. The fire Guardian's superorganized and intellectual. Not *artistic*, like me.

And that was really all makeup was, Hay Lin realized as she washed off layers of foundation. The face was the canvas, and the makeup was the paint!

When she returned to the bedroom, she turned off the TV and pulled out her art books and magazines. She found a few models with features similar to Taranee's—cocoa skin, dark brown eyes, roundish face.

She removed Taranee's wire-rimmed glasses and began to work, first matching one of the bottles of foundation to Taranee's skin color. Then she applied it to her face, to create the illusion of a perfect complexion.

She dusted Taranee's cheeks and forehead with powder to set the makeup. Next, she brushed on blusher. Then she put on an eye shadow that made Taranee's eyes look bigger and brighter. She applied black mascara and found a trendy, dark shade of lipstick.

"What do you think?" Hay Lin asked, handing Taranee the mirror.

Taranee grinned. "I look fantastic! But . . . don't you think this lipstick's too dark?"

Hay Lin laughed. "Let's try another. Then you can try doing mine again."

Fifteen minutes later, both Taranee and Hay Lin were completely made up.

"You look great!" Hay Lin exclaimed, admiring the final version of Taranee's face.

"Yep! We did it!" Taranee agreed. "You look great, too!"

Hay Lin checked the mirror. Her makeup *still* looked a little too heavy, but there was no time to fix it. When she checked her bedside clock, she realized they were going to be late.

"Let's get a move on," she said, leaping up from the bed. She grabbed her coat and shoved her feet into her shoes. "We've got to be there in five minutes!"

Halfway down the stairs, Taranee shouted, "Hang on a sec. . . . I've got to call my mom and tell her where I'm going."

Hay Lin stopped on the first floor. "Wait a

second! You're telling her *now*?"

Hay Lin had called home from school at lunchtime to ask permission to go out that night. She couldn't believe that Taranee had put off asking permission until the last minute. What if her mother said *no*?

"Come on," Hay Lin said. "I've already locked the upstairs door. Let's call her from the phone in the restaurant."

The girls ducked into the Silver Dragon. Hay Lin's mom was at the other end of the dining room, taking orders from the first customers of the evening. She had finished setting the empty tables with spotless linen and sparkling dishes. Normally, Hay Lin would have helped with that chore. Tonight, however, her parents had let her off the hook.

Hay Lin was overjoyed that her parents were so understanding. On most evenings and weekends, she pitched in at their restaurant, helping to clear tables, take phone orders, or watch the front register. Her mom and dad knew how hard Hay Lin worked, and when they could, they happily gave her the night off to have some fun.

Hay Lin hoped that Taranee's mom would

do the same. After all, Taranee worked 24-7 on getting good grades. She was one of Sheffield's top students. If anyone deserved a night off from studying, it was Taranee Cook.

Hay Lin leaned close to the phone so she could hear the conversation between Taranee and her mom.

"You won't be home for dinner because of an article?" She heard Judge Cook snap over the receiver. "May I know what article you're talking about?"

Taranee's brow grew furrowed with tension. "We have to write a report for school about the Rock and Roll Café," she answered, "and since they don't open until seven, we'll eat something there while we interview the owner, and then I'll come straight home."

"You should have told me earlier," Judge Cook scolded her. "It's already late!"

Hay Lin shook her head. Judge Cook sounded stern and cross.

It must be hard to have a mother who's a judge, Hay Lin thought. She's always pushing Taranee to do well in school, but why does she have to be so mean about it? I can't imagine my own mom being like that!

Hay Lin leaned close to Taranee again as Judge Cook's angry voice continued to pour from the phone. ". . . In any case, we'll talk it over at home. Now, go do the article," she snapped, "and no getting sidetracked on your way home!"

"*Yessss!* We did it!" Hay Lin squealed after Taranee hung up.

Taranee sighed heavily. "From the tone of her voice, I was worried we wouldn't."

"Come on! Let's hit the road! At lightning speed!" Hay Lin cried. The two girls raced for the back door to take a shortcut through the alley.

"Whoa! Slow down, girls!" Hay Lin's father cried.

As the two came barreling through the kitchen's double doors, they had run right into him. Surprised, he dropped a stack of take-out containers. *Plop!*

"Oops! Sorry, Dad!" Hay Lin cried, careful to keep her face down. "Running late! See you later!"

On most occasions, Hay Lin would have stopped to help her dad pick up the dropped containers, but this time she wasn't taking any chances. Her parents knew she was going to the Rock and Roll Café, but they didn't know about the makeup!

I love my glam new look, she thought, but I'm not so sure my mom and dad will!

FOUR

Will slammed shut her locker door in the changing room of the city pool building. *BANG!* "Like mother, like daughter," she muttered to herself, recalling her mom's earlier treatment of the living room phone.

Will still had no clue what her mother's problem was, but she had a first and last name for hers: *Mandy Anderson*!

Matt's girlfriend simply would not shut up! As they changed into their bathing suits, she jabbered away at Will as if they were old friends instead of the strangers they really were. Mostly, Will ignored her, but then a *real* friend of Will's from Sheffield's swim team joined the conversation.

". . . And it was the most embarrassing

moment of my life!" squealed Will's friend, a bubbly, freckle-faced girl with long curly hair.

Mandy laughed and grinned at the girl. "The first time I windsurfed was a nightmare for me, too! I was with a friend of mine. . . ."

Will rolled her eyes as she fell into step beside the two girls: they were now moving across the locker room, their flip-flops slapping against the clean tiles.

Go ahead, Mandy, Will thought, say *who* you were with the first time you windsurfed. It's obvious you're talking about *Matt*!

"The water was choppy, and he helped me stand up," Mandy continued. "When I finally managed, I tried to pull up the sail."

Will pictured Matt trying to help Mandy get up on a windsurfing board. She could just see the perfect sunny day, the blue water, the white sand, and the two of them laughing and joking with each other. In her mind, the scene was right out of a cheesy romantic comedy. *Hmmm,* Will thought, really glad to be a part of this. *Not!*

"But then this massive wave rolled in," Mandy went on, "and I fell down right on top of my friend!"

What a pathetic trick to get close to Matt, Will thought in disgust.

Mandy giggled. "So I decided to take up a different sport!"

"Yeah," Will muttered, "lucky for us—you took up swimming."

Stepping quickly, Will moved to get away from Miss I'm-Pretty-Good-at-Freestyle. The coach would be assembling the competitors any minute. Will needed to clear her head of Mandy's annoying laughter.

Will was one of eight girls from four different schools. Mr. Deplersun coached them all at the district level. Now he was testing his best swimmers for a spot at the upcoming citywide meet. And Will was determined to nail one of those prized spots—Mandy or no Mandy!

She'd worn her favorite white one-piece that night and brought her lucky green swim cap and blue goggles. She'd need the luck, too. She didn't know all of the girls the coach had assembled, but the few she did know were fantastic swimmers.

Sitting down at the edge of the pool, Will dipped her legs into the water to test the pool's temperature. It was lukewarm. Perfect, she thought. Taking a deep breath, the smell of chlorine tickled her nostrils; the distinctive aroma was familiar and comforting.

She swished her legs in the warm pool water and looked around. The benches for spectators were empty now, of course. The only sounds were the echoing laughter and chatter from the other seven competitors as they waited for the coach to begin their timed trial.

Will tried to imagine those stands on the day of the citywide meet. They would be completely full, with local news cameras set up to record every second of the action.

It'll be so exciting, Will thought as she tucked her shaggy red hair into her lucky swim cap. She imagined herself competing in the big meet, and a shiver went through her.

Calm down, Will! she advised herself. You haven't won a spot yet.

She took a deep breath and tried to focus on the upcoming swim. But her concentration was suddenly broken by Mandy's voice.

"So, why did you decide to take up swimming?" Mandy asked brightly.

Great, Will thought. She turned to find that Miss Charisma had plopped her tall, shapely form right next to her at the side of the pool.

Will looked away. "I . . . well . . . um . . ."

"Don't buy her act," Will's freckled friend cut in with a laugh as she passed behind them. "Out here, she's all shy, but in the pool she's ferocious!"

Normally, Will would have laughed at her friend's good-natured teasing. Tonight, however, she wasn't in the mood.

"I just like swimming, that's all," Will replied flatly.

"I'm going to get warmed up!" Will's friend announced. Then she leaned down, close to Will. "You know, your friend Mandy is really nice."

"What?" Will murmured. Mandy was *not* her friend.

"I'm glad you brought her here," the freckle-faced girl added before diving off the side of the pool.

Splash!

Oh, great, Will thought, watching ripples form in the blue water. As though taking Matt away from me wasn't enough. Now Mandy's stealing my friends, too.

"It was really nice of Matt to introduce us,"

Mandy told Will as she stuffed her long raven hair into her swim cap.

"Yeah," Will snapped, not meeting Mandy's eyes. "He's a real jewel." She continued looking away from the girl. Then a question occurred to her, and she turned to meet Mandy's pretty, long-lashed eyes.

"Have you known him for long?" Will asked.

Please say *no*, please say *no*, she found herself pleading silently. Maybe Matt really did love me once. Maybe I wasn't such a fool to fall for him.

Unfortunately, Mandy replied, "I've known Matt forever!" Then she gave a dreamy little sigh and added, "He's got a special place in my heart. And, believe me, if it wasn't for Matt, my life would *horrendible*!"

Horrendible's not even a word, Will thought furiously. Then she looked away from the girl again, feeling totally dejected.

Why did I even ask her that question? she thought. Why do I love to beat myself up like this?

"Everyone to the edge of the pool now!" The coach's deep voice echoed through the vast, glass-enclosed space, disrupting Will's thoughts and making her jump. "On the double!"

Will stood up, and Mandy followed as she took her place at the far end of the pool. The Olympic-size rectangle had been sectioned off into eight lanes. Numbered starting blocks marked each one. The coach directed Will to lane three and Mandy to lane four.

"And don't forget!" the coach bellowed, holding up his stopwatch. "Only one of you will make it to the finals!"

"Only one?" Will repeated in surprise. She'd assumed there was more than one spot! Now she realized just how much was riding on the next few minutes of freestyle strokes.

"Hey, you want to grab some pizza after this?" Mandy smiled at Will. "Loser buys!"

Man, I really am getting sick of her, Will thought. She steals Matt away from me, gets all buddy-buddy with my friends, and now she's totally wrecking my focus!

Not bothering to answer, Will stepped onto her starting block and slipped her blue goggles on. But she didn't feel ready to compete. The weight of Matt's betrayal had left her drained and tired. Her limbs seemed heavy as she bent slightly forward, getting into the starting position. Her posture was off, and her breathing was way too shallow.

Come on, she told herself, block everything out, *concentrate*! She took a few deep breaths and imagined that the blue pool was a vast sky, stretching out in front of her. Then she zeroed in on her small piece of it—the single line of lane three.

"On your marks!" the coach shouted.

It's just you and the water, Will told herself. It's just you and that long line of blue.

"Get your wallet ready!"

Mandy's chipper teasing from the next block suddenly shattered Will's concentration again.

Will was furious. Squeezing her eyes shut, she made a decision. All right, Mandy, she thought, I've just about had it! If only one of us can make it, it's not going to be you!

"Get set!" the coach warned.

Will took a deep breath. She bent her knees, coiling her muscles, preparing to spring. But something else was coiled inside of her, too, something powerful and supernatural, and it was also ready to spring.

"Go!" the coach roared.

Splash!

Seven competitors dived headfirst into the blue pool. *One* slipped off her starting block.

"Oops!" Mandy cried.

As Will sliced through the water, she heard the coach bellowing angrily, "What are you doing, Mandy? You weak in the knees today?"

"How weird," Mandy said to the coach as she quickly climbed the block again. "That's never happened to me before!"

Will heard the second splash and knew Mandy was finally in the water, well behind her. Good, she thought: Mandy can take everything else, but the place in the finals is mine!

Will felt lighter than ever now. She felt as though she were flying, as though she had her Guardian wings! Her legs were pumping, her arms moving her quickly through the clear, warm blue.

She saw the wall coming up and executed a perfect underwater turnaround: somersaulting gracefully, she used her legs to push off the far side of the pool.

One more pool length! she told herself. I've got to do it! I've got to!

Her breathing came harder, her heart beat more furiously as she propelled herself forward.

Stroke, stroke, stroke! Kick, kick, kick!

Finally, she reached the end. Gasping for breath, she ripped off her goggles. Her eyes sought the coach. He was pointing at her and nodding.

"Lane three! Will Vandom!"

"Yesssss!" Will tore off her lucky swim cap and waved it in the air.

Less than a minute later, the other girls were climbing out of the pool.

"Nice going, Will," they cried.

"Good luck in the finals!"

"See that?" Will's freckled friend joked to another competitor, helping her out of the water. "Will did it again! In the pool she's a shark, and on dry land she's a little angel!"

Mandy walked up to Will. The bounce had left her step, but her smile was still there. "Looks like I owe you a pizza," she said.

"Nah," said Will, fluffing out her damp red hair. "You don't owe me anything."

"Congratulations, Will," the coach said, offering her a firm handshake. "You had the right stuff today!"

"Thanks, sir!" Will replied excitedly.

Will's friend rushed up to her. "Aren't you going to congratulate me? I kept my usual last place!"

Mandy laughed at that one, though the coach frowned.

"Mandy Anderson!" he said sharply. "You've got nothing to laugh about."

"But I came in second—" Mandy began to reply.

The coach cut her off. "Are you telling me that you're satisfied with your performance?"

I am! Will thought.

"No, Mr. Deplersun," Mandy told the coach. "But something strange happened. I couldn't manage to get off the diving platform, and then I slipped. It sounds impossible, but it's true."

Will suppressed a smile. Not as impossible as you think, she muttered to herself.

"Don't make excuses," the coach scolded. "With that sloppy start, you blew your chance at the finals."

Mandy's usually bright eyes finally dimmed. She hung her head. "I know, and I'm sorry. . . ."

"As for you," the coach boomed, pointing his finger at Will, "you'll come here to train every day. I want you in better shape than you've ever been!"

Will grinned and nodded. She was more than ready to put the past behind her and face the challenges ahead.

FIVE

Peter Cook was happy. He had finished up his homework early and had had time to browse the Internet for some cool new downloads. Music was his thing. And as he turned off the computer, he smelled something delicious cooking downstairs.

"Mmmm," he murmured, getting up to head for the kitchen.

With his hands in his pockets, he strolled down the second-floor hallway. On the way, he popped his head into Taranee's bedroom.

"That's weird," he murmured.

Peter's little sister was usually hard at work before dinner, getting a head start on her homework or reviewing old notes. But tonight, Taranee's bedroom was empty.

Shrugging, Peter closed her bedroom door and went downstairs. Humming to himself, he followed the tantalizing aroma of Italian pasta sauce through the dining room. At the entrance to the kitchen, he leaned his lanky body against the door frame and watched his parents cooking together.

His dad was hard at work, wearing a white apron with his shirtsleeves rolled up. His mom was all business as she put a pot of water on the stove.

Peter smiled and wagged his finger at his mother. "Your Honor," he teased, "I find you guilty!"

Judge Cook glanced over her shoulder at her son. Sometimes she loosened up at Peter's teasing, but not this time. From the expression on her face, she appeared totally stressed.

"Don't start with me," she said. Then she turned back to the stove.

Whoa, Peter thought, Mom must have had a hard day today in court. One thing Peter had come to learn about his mother was to read the signs she gave off . . . and how to stay out of trouble when she looked as mad as she did now.

Deep down, Peter knew his mom really loved her family and wanted what was best for them. Her fiery temper, however, was sometimes hard to take.

Peter was more like his easygoing dad. With his black dreadlocks (tied back in a ponytail), that red goatee, and killer smile, he believed that relaxed charm got you a lot further than pushy attitude. And a mellower spirit was a truly effective shield against the daggers of stressed-out fury.

When his mom showed anger, Peter would deflect it like a Teflon martial artist. He wished Taranee could have learned how to handle their mom that way, but she was just too stubborn. In many ways, Taranee's temper was a lot like their mother's.

Instead of trying to charm their mom out of her stern judge persona, Taranee would bristle and argue. Mother and daughter always ended up fighting instead of reconciling.

Maybe my mother and sister are just too much alike, Peter decided. It was hard to miss the similarities between them. Both females were highly intelligent and very headstrong. At times in the Cook household, that combination could be extremely combustible!

All the more reason for the cool calm of my own personal touch! Peter figured. And for sure, whatever's bugging Mom tonight, she definitely needs my help in lightening up.

Sauntering casually across the kitchen, Peter continued his teasing. "This woman has been caught red-handed!" he exclaimed. "After a hard day of work, she's making her son's favorite gnocchi. That's just not fair!" He puckered up and gave his mom a big kiss on the cheek. "Thanks, Mom," he said sweetly.

Judge Cook shook her head of blunt-cut black hair. "When you smooch me like that, it means you're hiding something," she said accusingly.

"Then I guess you better find me guilty," he joked.

"No," his mom said. She turned from the stove and shook her wooden spoon at him. "Instead, you can tell me about the Rock and Roll Café. What do you know about it?"

Peter laughed. "Aha! . . . So, you're planning a nice little evening out?" He turned to his father and winked. "What do you say, Dad? Should we give her permission?"

Peter's father nodded and laughed.

"I asked you a question!" Peter's mom cut in, waving her spoon like a gavel.

"I realize that, Your Honor," Peter said, bowing theatrically, "and I have the answer."

"Well?" his mom asked, folding her arms in front of her.

"The Rock and Roll Café is a lively little hangout," said Peter describing it as smoothly as a disc jockey would have on air. "It's where the Heatherfield crowd gets together to spend cheerful evenings together in good company."

"And that's all?" Peter's mom asked.

Smiling, Peter cleared his throat and continued. "At the café, they serve one hundred and twenty kinds of sandwiches, one hundred and twelve kinds of french fries, a hundred and three different soft drinks—not to mention their fantastic happy hour. Complete with good—no, *great*—music!"

Peter's mom nodded. "Okay, Peter," she said. "I get the picture."

Peter snatched a carrot off the counter and munched on it. He didn't know why his mom was so interested in the Rock and Roll Café, but he thought of one more thing to add: "Opens at seven, closed on Tuesdays."

"Whaaat?!" screeched his mother.

Peter froze in midmunch. Uh-oh. What had he said? In an instant, his mother's face had gone from showing the beginnings of a smile to grimacing furiously.

Peter's dad seemed just as surprised as Peter at Judge Cook's sudden transformation. He walked across the kitchen and put a warm hand on his wife's shoulder. "What's wrong, Theresa?" he asked.

"I'll tell you what's wrong!" she replied, flaring up. "Your daughter lied! Today is Tuesday, and if that place is closed, I'd very much like to know where she's gone!"

Peter closed his eyes and rubbed his forehead. His cool, carefree attitude was officially shattered as he realized what he'd done.

What a *moron* you are, Peter! he told himself. Couldn't you have just kept your mouth shut?

His sister was a top student at Sheffield. She always worked hard, and she was a good, considerate kid. The last thing Peter wanted to do was get her into trouble.

I don't know where she went tonight, he

thought, but I can guess who she's with . . . Nigel.

In Peter's estimation, Taranee's boyfriend was a really nice guy. Whatever Taranee was up to with him, it was probably completely innocent. Peter's mother, however, would never see it that way. And Peter had to admit, she had a pretty good reason to be wary. In her role as a judge, she had sentenced Nigel for the crime of breaking and entering. Security guards had caught him inside the Heatherfield Museum one night, along with two troublemakers named Uriah and Kurt.

According to Taranee, however, Nigel wasn't like those other two thugs. And after serving his community-service sentence, he had distanced himself from them. Finally, his crush on Taranee had led him to ask her out. Now he appeared to be a model kid.

Peter remembered Taranee's coming to him one afternoon for advice. "How do you know if a boy actually likes you?" she'd asked.

Peter had almost laughed out loud at Taranee's question. When he saw the serious expression on her face, however, he had stifled his chuckles.

Taranee had told him about a wonderful thing that Nigel had done for her at school. She was supposed to be photographing insects for her biology class, and Nigel had caught a butterfly for her. He'd put it in a box with her name on it, and he'd left it as a present for her to find.

Peter had been astonished to hear the story. He had known right away that the boy had it bad for his sister. "There's no mystery as far as this guy's feelings," he'd told Taranee. "Nigel definitely likes you."

Peter's mom was not nearly as understanding. She had been livid at the very idea of her only daughter dating a lawbreaker. But Peter and his father had convinced the judge to ease up on her criticism of Nigel. The boy had, after all, completed his community service. And Taranee really liked him—which was reason enough, in Peter's view, to give the guy a chance.

Peter was thrilled when his mom finally allowed Taranee to go out with Nigel. Things had been going really well, too, until tonight.

Sighing again, Peter gave himself another mental kick.

The last thing I ever wanted to do was blow Taranee's cover, he thought. If anyone's earned an innocent night out, it's my little sis. I just wish Mom felt the same!

But it didn't look like that wish would be coming true anytime soon.

"Wait until I get a hold of that girl!" Peter's mom said, pacing up and down the kitchen floor. "Just wait!"

SIX

My first double date! Taranee thought. This is so fantastic.

She and Nigel were walking hand in hand beside Hay Lin and Eric. The sun had completely set, and Heatherfield's streetlights glowed golden in the violet twilight. With the rush hour over, street traffic had lessened, and the crowds on the sidewalks had thinned.

The city seems so much more magical in the evening, Taranee thought. And so much more romantic!

On the sidewalks around them, young people laughed in small groups. And couples strolled arm in arm, whispering to each other on their way to romantic dinners.

Just like us! Taranee thought. Okay, she

admitted, so Nigel and I are not *officially* on a double date with Hay Lin and Eric. We are really on assignment for the school newspaper. But it's close enough!

A year earlier, Taranee could only have fantasized about holding a boy's hand or going to a popular nightclub. Imagining anything close to it had made her shiver with shyness. But now that she and Nigel were friends, everything had changed, even her old insecurities.

Up ahead, the Rock and Roll Café beckoned. Taranee couldn't wait to see the inside of the place. Her older brother, Peter, had been there many times. He'd talked about how cool the restaurant was and how there was always good music playing there.

As Taranee moved closer to the café with her friends, she noticed that something was wrong. The marquee over the restaurant, featuring the image of a huge guitar and red letters spelling out *Rock and Roll Café* in neon lights, was dark.

Suddenly, Taranee got a bad feeling in the pit of her stomach. She glanced anxiously at Hay Lin, and then the girls rushed up to the café's entrance, with the boys right on their heels.

"Oh, no! It can't be!" Taranee cried.

A "Closed" sign hung on the club's glass-front door, along with another sign listing the café's regular hours. The place was open every day *but* Tuesday!

"Ace reporters, aren't we?" Eric muttered.

Nigel sighed. "Maybe we should have called first."

"What a disaster!" Hay Lin exclaimed.

"We had to pick the *one* day it's closed to do the story," Nigel said, shaking his head.

Hay Lin stared at the sign. "Let's look on the bright side. We got our first piece of information. We'll start the article by recommending that people *not* come here on Tuesdays."

Nigel laughed. "Nice beginning, but I think we'll need more than that."

"Do you have any ideas?" Taranee asked, putting a hand on her hip.

Nigel threw her a teasing smile. "Don't worry. If you can't do it, I'll write your part."

Taranee couldn't speak for a moment, looking into Nigel's warm brown eyes. He was wearing a new turtleneck sweater, and the shade almost perfectly matched the light brown color of his chin-length hair. He looked really cute.

And Taranee knew that he felt the same way about her. Earlier, when he'd first seen her new "glam" face, complete with eyeliner and lipstick, he'd stared speechlessly at her for a full minute!

"You look nice," he'd finally told her softly. "Really nice."

"Thanks!" she'd said. Then he'd taken her hand, and Taranee had thought she could never have been any happier.

Seeing Nigel like that, so sweet and warm, she could hardly believe he was the same boy who had once been an Outfielder.

As a member of Uriah's gang, Nigel had resided on Sheffield's antisocial fringes. He'd gotten into trouble by behaving badly and pulling nasty pranks like entangling all the bikes on the school rack or bullying the so-called "geeky" kids like Martin Tubbs. Uriah had even targeted Taranee. It was Nigel who'd made him stop.

Falling for Taranee had really helped Nigel turn his life around. He had dropped out of Uriah's gang. And he'd actually joined a couple of school activities—like the newspaper, which was what had brought them out to the Rock and Roll Café that very night.

He'd become a much better student, too. He and Taranee had started studying together in the school library. The effort was slowly improving his grades.

Unfortunately, Taranee knew that her mom still didn't trust Nigel. Judge Cook believed Taranee was too good for him, just because one time he had been caught breaking in to the Heatherfield Museum.

But my mother doesn't know the real truth! Taranee thought. As the fire Guardian, I've been an even bigger lawbreaker than Nigel!

In order to go through a portal to Metamoor, Taranee had broken in to the very same museum that Nigel had entered illegally. She'd committed more "unlawful entries" by getting inside Elyon's abandoned house when she wasn't supposed to. And she'd broken in to the Heatherfield Observatory, which she had *also* trashed, while fighting a supernaturally ugly dog-beast!

There was no way Taranee could tell her mother about her life as a Guardian. So she had to persuade her mom to trust Nigel for the same reason she did—because he was special.

When I'm with Nigel, Taranee thought, I don't have to be a super student or a super any-thing. I can simply be me, and, well . . . *happy*!

Nigel made Taranee feel *good* about herself. He valued her for who she was—not for the grades she brought home or the college she would attend someday. Nigel allowed Taranee just to relax and take life as it came.

Even now, standing on the sidewalk in front of the Rock and Roll Café, Nigel made Taranee feel as though everything would be okay—despite the fact that their assignment was a bust!

"So what do we do?" Taranee asked, point-ing to the closed café. "We won't have anything to bring to the newsroom tomorrow."

"Wrong!" Hay Lin cried. "We'll take a walk around the city."

"And?" Taranee pressed.

"And the great article 'Heatherfield by Night' will write itself!" Hay Lin waved her arm theatrically at the twinkling skyscrapers rising above them.

Eric grinned. "Hay Lin, that's a great idea! You're a genius!"

Taranee nodded. She had to agree. Before

they'd even arrived at the café, she'd already been noticing how magical the city felt at night!

BAAANG!

The sudden noise was loud and violent, like a sledgehammer hitting the side of a car. Taranee, Nigel, Hay Lin, and Eric automatically wheeled around to see where the noise had come from.

"Oh, no . . ." Nigel murmured.

Taranee gasped.

Across the street, right near a newsstand, Uriah was kicking a soda machine—hard.

Bang! Bang! BANG!

In the building above the machine, an old woman peered out her window. She didn't say anything, but she looked upset and scared.

"Stupid machine!" Uriah shouted. "It ate my money!"

"Ha, ha, ha!" laughed Uriah's chubby friend Kurt. "Kick it in! That'll learn it!"

"I don't believe this," Nigel muttered.

Before Taranee could stop him, he took off heading for his old gang leader. "What are you doing, Uriah?" he called as he jogged across the street. "Cut it out!"

Uriah turned. "Nigel? What did you say to

me?" The gangly, pimply-faced boy was standing directly beneath a streetlight. His orange hair appeared to glow, the gelled spikes looking like flames.

"I said, 'Cut it out,'" Nigel repeated.

Uriah's orange eyebrows rose. He shot Kurt an amused look. Then he leaned against the side of the newly dented soda machine.

"You're not my mother," he told Nigel. "You can't tell me what to do."

"I'm not your mother," Nigel replied, "but I was your *friend*. And I don't want to see you get into even more trouble."

Taranee didn't know what to do. She quickly crossed the street with Eric and Hay Lin. All three of them stood watching as Nigel and Uriah exchanged heated words. Finally, Eric stepped up.

"Come on, Nigel," he said, grabbing him by the shoulders. "He's not worth it."

Uriah waved his hands at them. "I won't even answer you. You're a nobody, Nigel. Go and take your walk with your pathetic little friends."

"Leave them out of this!" Nigel replied angrily.

Uriah snickered like an evil little imp. "Oh, sorry," he said sarcastically, "I didn't *mean* to *offend* them. I wouldn't dream of hurting the feelings of the school nerd—"

He pointed at Taranee, but she didn't care.

Uriah's a total jerk, she thought. Who cares what he thinks of me or anyone else?

"And why would I want to offend our beautiful Metal Mouth here?" Uriah added as he smugly gestured toward Hay Lin.

Eric suddenly released his hold on Nigel. "What did you call her?" he demanded, stepping right up to the orange-haired boy.

Uriah just laughed.

"Apologize to her, now!" Eric cried, pushing Uriah in the shoulder to make his point.

Uriah held his ground. He looked Eric up and down. "What have we here?" he taunted. "A fearless knight in shining armor?"

Kurt stepped forward, clenching his meaty fists. He was obviously getting ready to pounce on Eric.

Nigel blocked his path. "You stay out of this," he warned.

Taranee turned to notice that Hay Lin's cheeks had flushed red. Uriah's comment had hit hard. "He's just a creep, Hay Lin," Taranee said gently. "Don't let him get to you!"

"My braces are beautiful!" Hay Lin insisted. Staring down at the concrete sidewalk, she swallowed hard, as if tears were welling up inside. "He shouldn't say things like that!"

Now Eric and Uriah were nose to nose, their puffed-up chests nearly touching.

"I said, *apologize to her*!" Eric demanded.

Uriah's eyes narrowed. "And I said, *Metal Mouth*!"

"You're begging for a black eye, Uriah!" Eric said threateningly.

Taranee didn't know what to do. The situation was quickly spiraling out of control. Eric was taller than Uriah. But Uriah was a lot meaner. Anything could happen if a fight really started.

The fire Guardian knew she wasn't supposed to use her powers in public, but she considered this an emergency! With a deep breath, she gave Hay Lin a meaningful look.

"It's our turn now," she whispered. "Don't you think?"

Hay Lin nodded eagerly. "You got that right," she said, as a payback smile beautifully revealed her W.I.T.C.H. braces.

"Air!" Hay Lin declared.

"Arrrrrgggh!" Uriah cried as a ferocious burst of wind literally blew him away.

Eric Lyndon stared in confusion as Uriah whirled away from him.

"Fire!" Taranee announced.

"Ouch!" Kurt shouted. "My feet are burning! Ouch!"

Now it was Nigel's turn to gawk at Kurt. The kid was hopping around as if he were trying to walk barefoot on a barbecue.

However, before any of the boys could ask what was going on, sirens could be heard screaming down the city street.

WEEEOOOO! WEEEOOOO! WEEEOOOO!

"The police!" Taranee cried, seeing two Heatherfield patrol cars barreling toward them.

WEEEOOOO! WEEEOOOO! WEEEOOOO!

We shouldn't have stuck around to use our powers! She thought, glancing worriedly at Hay Lin. We should have just gotten out of here!

It was too late to flee, however. The patrol cars had just screeched to a stop right in front of them.

Taranee tried not to panic as the officers

climbed out of their vehicles. She tried to imagine what her mother, the judge, would have said if she had been there.

I've *got* to talk our way out of this, Taranee thought, approaching the policemen. After all, Uriah and Kurt are the lawbreakers here. Once I explain everything, I'm sure the officers will arrest those jerks and let the rest of us go.

I hope.

SEVEN

By the time Will got home from swimming, she was *starving*. All she'd eaten since noon was one protein bar.

As soon as she opened the front door, she raced straight for the kitchen. She was ready to devour every last leftover in the fridge. But her mother stopped her.

Putting a hand over Will's eyes, her mom led her into the next room. "Ta-da!" she sang.

Will opened her eyes to find a huge surprise. The dinner table was draped with white linen and decorated with glowing candlesticks. Delicious smells wafted out from under covered dishes. And her mom's boyfriend, Mr. Collins, was standing there, clapping.

Mr. Collins was not just her mom's boyfriend, he was also Will's history teacher. He was still wearing the same white shirt and blue slacks she'd seen him in earlier that day at school. He'd loosened his red tie. And beneath his bushy brown mustache, he wore a big grin.

At once, Will realized what was happening. Right after she'd won the swim trials, she had called her mom from the pool to tell her the good news. Obviously, her mom had arranged a quick celebration dinner. She must have simply warmed up the food she had made earlier and called Mr. Collins to come over and join them.

Will thought the gesture was supersweet and everything, but she was *still* totally *famished*! After saying a quick hello to Mr. Collins, she sat down and dug right in to the food. By the time Will's mom filled their water glasses, Will was halfway through her steak and a giant baked potato.

"I'd like to propose a toast," Mr. Collins announced raising his glass. "To our very own future champion!"

Will's mom grinned and raised her glass, too. "To Will."

Will gulped. Mr. Collins and her mom had caught her off guard. Her mouth was stuffed with food at the moment, and her cheeks were bulging like a chipmunk's!

"And I'm sorry if I wasn't paying too much attention to you earlier today," her mom continued, clinking her own glass against Will's. "I had a lot on my mind."

Will quickly chewed and swallowed the food in her mouth. "No problem," she finally said.

"You've always been so dedicated to swimming," added Mr. Collins, rising from his seat and extending his glass across the table. "I'm happy you made the finals."

More than dedicated, Will thought, touching her glass to his. She thought of that little bit of magic she had used in order to seal her win against Mandy. *Helped out* is what I'd call it, Will told herself, but that's good enough for me!

Will sat down again and smiled, surprised she was feeling so good. The whole Matt situation had totally sunk her spirits—and her appetite—lately.

Things sure can turn around fast, she thought, shoving another forkful of baked potato into her mouth. It's funny how often life can be like that. One part will fall totally to pieces just as another comes together.

Like Mr. Collins and mom, she added silently.

At one time, Will had absolutely loathed the idea of her mother's dating her history teacher. She remembered the first time she'd seen them together. They were having lunch at an outdoor café when Will and her friends had walked by.

Will had been completely humiliated when Cornelia pointed them out. How could my mom do this? Will had wondered at the time. How could she totally embarrass me by dating my teacher?

She and her mom had had a big fight about it. As time went by, however, Will's objections had lessened. Her fights with her mom weren't so much about Mr. Collins anymore but about her mom's always being too busy for Will. She was either at work or on a date, and she never had time, even when Will needed her most.

Then, things changed, and it was her mom's turn. She was the one who became angry, because *Will* was never around. What with best friends, school, Matt, and her duties as

Keeper of the Heart, Will no longer had time for her mom.

Will wanted to believe that all that drama was behind them now.

Things are definitely getting better, she thought. Today proves it! Mom actually *listened* to me earlier when I told her how important swimming was to me. She lifted my grounding punishment so I could go to the tryouts. Then she arranged this great last-minute celebration dinner!

Will didn't even mind that Mr. Collins was there. In fact, she was kind of glad he'd come. He made it more of a party. Plus, she had to admit, he was a supernice guy. He really cared about her mom. And Will wanted her mother to be happy.

After everything she's been through, Will thought, she totally deserves some bliss!

Will remembered how wound up her mother had been earlier in the day. The anonymous phone calls and the beautiful fresh roses thrown in the garbage were still a mystery. At this moment, however, her mom appeared to have forgotten about all that. And that was just fine with Will.

DING-DONG!

"Oh!" Will's mom said. "That must be our neighbor. She wanted to bring us some of her organic oranges."

"Well, I'm not getting it," Will declared. "I can't handle another one of her lessons about houseplants and gardening!"

The woman who lived a few doors away was really into growing her own herbs, fruits, and vegetables. She had flower boxes and house-plants in every room of her apartment.

One weekend, she'd hired Will to water her plants while she was away. How hard could it be to trickle water into a few pots? Will had thought at the time, and she had accepted the task without a second thought. But there were well over one hundred pots! It had taken her ninety minutes to finish the job.

Will's mother stood up and took hold of Mr. Collins's arm. "Let's *all* go answer the door *together*," she said, pulling him up.

"What! Why?" he cried, resisting. "I'm not interested in a lesson on gardening, either!"

DING-DONG! DING-DONG!

Will couldn't help laughing at the funny face Mr. Collins was making.

"But if she sees we have a guest," Will's mom argued, "maybe she won't stay long."

"Sorry," Mr. Collins said. "You're on your own!"

DING-DONG! DING-DONG!

Will's mom put her hands on her hips and glared at the two of them. Will and Mr. Collins exchanged a conspiratorial look. In unison, they shook their heads, refusing to budge.

Finally, Will's mom threw up her hands. "Chickens!" she exclaimed, heading for the door herself.

Behind her, Will and Mr. Collins burst into laughter.

"Hey, cut it out!" Will's mom called back to them as she walked across the apartment. "Act serious, you two!"

That only made it worse. Mr. Collins doubled over. And Will began cackling so hard she ended up on the floor, beating the carpet with her fist. "Ha-ha-ha! Hee-hee-hee!"

Will's mom was still shaking her head when she opened the door and gasped.

The person standing there wasn't the plant-loving neighbor. This visitor was a tall, handsome, older man. He wore a yellow vest over a white shirt, and a green jacket and slacks. He held a present wrapped in purple paper. And his hair was bright red, streaked with silver.

"Susan!" the man exclaimed.

Will's laughter had immediately ceased when her mother gasped. So had her teacher's. Now they walked to the front door and flanked Will's mother, who had grown alarmingly pale.

"Tell me this isn't happening," Will's mom murmured.

The visitor's gaze shifted. "Will!" he exclaimed with a big smile.

Will blinked. She could tell the man was waiting for her to react somehow, but she just stood there, unable to say anything.

The man furrowed his already wrinkled brow. "Will . . ." he said, stepping forward, "don't you recognize me?"

Will stared into brown eyes that looked curiously like her own. And the man's hair . . . Will realized that, except for the silver, it was exactly the same shade as her own. She took a closer look at the man's features and gasped. He was a lot older than she remembered him, but she *did* remember him.

"It's your father," the man said, confirming

what she'd just realized. "I'm back!"

Will's jaw slackened. *Back?* she thought. What does he mean, *back?*

"And this time, it's for good!" he promised.

Will could see that her mom was far from happy about her former husband's sudden reappearance. Mrs. Vandom had begun to frown, and her fists were clenched in balls of fury.

"What . . . what are you doing here?" she demanded.

Will's father scratched his head. "I was hoping for a warmer welcome, Susan. Did I interrupt something, by chance?"

For a long, uncomfortable moment, the three adults stood staring at one another. Poor Mr. Collins looked as confused as Will felt. He didn't utter a word.

My gosh! What a weird scene, Will thought. Can you say, *awkward?*

Finally, Will's mother spoke again. "I asked you a question, Thomas. What are you doing here? What do you want from us?"

"Calm down, Susan!" Will's father replied. "I just want to talk to you . . . and to Will. I have a lot of things to tell you, and I want to, need to, make up for everything—"

Will's mother cut him off. "You've got a lot of nerve showing up here after all this time! A lot of nerve!"

"Please, Susan!" Will's father cried. "A bit of civility, would you?" He gestured toward Mr. Collins. "Seeing as we have a visitor."

Omigosh, Will thought. I wonder how Mr. Collins feels about being caught up in all this!

"How dare you?" Will's mom screeched. "*We* don't have a visitor. And the only person who doesn't belong here is *you*!"

Will looked closely at Mr. Collins. If he felt any discomfort or embarrassment at the situation, he was doing a good job of hiding it.

"Don't worry, Susan," he gently said. "Maybe I should leave you all alone."

Will's mother pulled Mr. Collins aside. They spoke quietly for a moment. Then Mr. Collins retrieved his coat and hat and headed out.

Will's dad looked almost smug as he held the door. "I appreciate your discretion," he told Mr. Collins. "You know, this being a little family reunion and all."

Will's mom stood seething as Will's father closed the door. Before she could rip into him, however, he turned away and smiled at Will.

"Will!" he cried. "How you've grown! The last time I saw you, you were so little!"

"You *would have* seen her grow up," Will's mom angrily pointed out, "if you hadn't gone and left us!"

Will's dad ignored her mom. Instead, he turned back to Will and held out the big purple box in his hands. "This is for you, sweetheart," he said.

Will stood with her arms folded, feeling torn up inside. Her mom was obviously furious that her dad was there. On the other hand, her dad was being really friendly and sweet, and she hadn't seen him in a very long time.

Not sure what to say or do, Will glanced from her mom to her dad to the big purple box. "Do I have to open it?" she asked uncertainly.

Her dad laughed. "What do you mean?" he said, pushing the present into her hands. "Of course you do!"

Will stared at her father, studying his hair, his eyes, his face. She couldn't help it. It was weird to see him again after so long.

Before they'd moved to Heatherfield, Will's mom had hidden away every last photo of him. She wanted no reminders. That was one reason

Will hadn't recognized him at first.

He seems so different from what I remember, she thought. Then again, I'm different, too— and in more ways than my dad could *ever* guess! Do you want to know what's *really* happened to me since you last saw me? she wanted to ask him. I became a Guardian. As Keeper of the Heart, I learned to lead my best friends. I fought the creatures of Metamoor, defeated a supernatural sorceress, and saved the known universe!

It was all so fantastic, Will knew he'd never believe it.

Maybe someday I'll be able to tell him the truth, Will thought. Maybe someday my *whole* family will learn all about the real me . . . and be totally proud.

That someday wasn't today, however. Will couldn't begin to guess what her mother was feeling about her dad's showing up after all this time. Will wasn't even sure about how she herself felt toward him.

However, she *was* curious about what kind of gift he'd brought for her. She turned the package over in her hands. The box was big but not very heavy.

She started to tear the paper, when her mother pounced.

"Don't unwrap that package, Will!" she cried. "I forbid you."

Will's dad stepped between them. "It's just a little present, Susan," he said softly. "A harmless, innocent present."

Will froze, staring at her parents. Finally, her mother nodded, and Will began to unwrap the gift. When she glimpsed what was inside, she was genuinely surprised.

Wow! Will thought as she took the gift out of the box. A stuffed green frog with a goofy little grin peered at her. He remembered that I love frogs, Will said to herself.

She looked up at her mother. She had never seen her so angry.

Will was now more confused than ever. Shouldn't her dad's returning with a really sweet gift be a happy occasion? Shouldn't she feel better about seeing him?

But somehow the mood was not calm or happy. Will gave the frog a hug and hoped that things would change . . . for the better.

EIGHT

Taranee sat at a table with Nigel, Hay Lin, and Eric, but it wasn't a table at the Rock and Roll Café.

There was no live music where she was sitting. There were no waitresses or menus, either. That was because Taranee was continuing her unofficial double date in Interrogation Room B of Heatherfield's midtown police precinct!

The room where Taranee now sat wasn't exactly what she'd have called romantic. Its walls were a dull shade of green, and the floor was scuffed. The only window in the room looked out on to the hallway. And the table where they sat was banged up and stained with coffee-cup rings.

Uriah and Kurt were sitting there, too.

Taranee was furious. In her view, Uriah and Kurt deserved to be there, but she and her friends did not!

Earlier, when the police first arrived on the scene, Taranee had tried to talk herself and her friends out of trouble. She'd calmly explained to the arresting officers what had happened and all about Uriah's bad track record.

It appeared they hadn't cared. And they hadn't seemed to care that her mother was Judge Cook, either. They'd just herded all the kids into their two patrol cars and driven them to the station house.

The next thing Taranee knew, she and her friends were locked in this less-than-lovely interrogation room and told to wait. For nearly thirty minutes, they sat. At last, the precinct captain stomped in and started yelling at the top of his lungs.

Taranee was stunned. The captain hadn't given them a chance to talk or tell their side of the story. He hadn't bothered to ask them one question! He had just listened to and sided with the old woman who had called in about a disturbance outside her window. Then he had started yelling. Talk about unfair punishment.

"You all must be pleased with your little stunt!" he raged. Then he pointed at Taranee and Hay Lin. "And what have you got all over your faces? I'm talking to you, girls!"

Taranee bristled. By now, she was practically channeling her mother's indignation. I don't believe this guy, she thought. First, he stomps all over our rights. Then he pretends to be a fashion critic. What does our makeup have to do with anything that happened?

"Instead of spending your evenings raising a ruckus," the captain said, "you should be dedicating yourselves to your studies!"

Behind her round, wire-rimmed glasses, Taranee's eyes narrowed. Finally, she spoke up. "With all due respect," she told the captain, "that's *exactly* what we were trying to do!"

"Funny," the captain replied, "I got the impression it was just the *opposite*."

"Well, you got the *wrong* impression," Taranee assured him.

Just then, Taranee noticed another officer walking by the observation window. "Good night, Captain Coletti!" the man called, glancing into the room.

Taranee thought that the second officer

looked really familiar. Before she could figure out why, Captain Coletti shut the door and got on her case again.

"You're just trying to duck the truth," he said, accusingly.

"The truth?" Was this guy kidding? Maybe he should try looking up the word *ironic*. "Before throwing the book at somebody," Taranee added, full of attitude, "maybe you should check your *facts!*"

The captain scowled. "You'll shut your mouth if you know what's good for you, little girl!"

"Shut my mouth?" Taranee balled her hands in fists. She could feel the fire rising inside her. "How dare you?"

Beside her, Hay Lin shifted uncomfortably in her chair. "Calm down, Taranee," she whispered softly.

The fire Guardian wasn't sure how much more she could take before the situation really got too hot to handle. Luckily, she never got the chance to find out. Suddenly, the door to the room swung open. In walked the officer who'd just passed by their observation window moments earlier.

"Hey, Captain," the officer said, "you can go now. I'll take care of this. I know these kids."

With a start, Taranee realized why the man looked so familiar to her. A closer look at his face revealed him to be Irma Lair's father!

Captain Coletti stepped out of the room with Officer Lair. A few minutes later, Irma's father came back alone.

That nasty captain can count himself lucky, Taranee thought, because when I lose my cool, it's no joke!

Officer Lair was much nicer to the kids than his captain had been. Instead of lecturing them as if they'd just been featured on TV's *Ten Most Wanted*, he sat down with them as if they were guests in his home.

Taranee quickly realized that Captain Coletti's status as a stranger had its advantages. His little lecture may have been annoying, but explaining everything to her friend's father turned out to be really, really, *really* embarrassing!

An hour later, Taranee sat down next to Nigel in the station house waiting room—which was no more romantic than the interrogation room.

Hay Lin and Eric sat next to Taranee on one

hard bench, while Uriah and Kurt rested like dejected lumps on another. After a few minutes, Nigel got up and started pacing between them.

Officer Lair had telephoned all of their parents. Now it was just a waiting game, to see who would show up first.

Eric's grandfather arrived first. Professor Lyndon didn't say much. He simply motioned for Eric to follow him out.

Eric squeezed Hay Lin's hand. He waved to Taranee and Nigel, glared at Uriah and Kurt, and left.

Taranee sighed and slid closer to Hay Lin on the bench. Nigel continued to pace.

Ten minutes later, Hay Lin's mother showed up. As soon as Hay Lin saw her walk into the room, tears formed in her eyes. "I'm so sorry," she sobbed.

Hay Lin's mother opened her arms, and Hay Lin ran to her. Mother and daughter stood in the middle of the room, hugging each other in silence.

At last, Hay Lin's mother spoke. "When the police called us, what a scare we had," she said, patting Hay Lin's long, dark pigtails. "Do you have any idea?"

"I'm sorry, Mom," Hay Lin repeated. "I really am so sorry. It won't happen again."

"Good," her mother said. "And I hope you don't get any more of these crazy ideas into your head." She sighed and released her daughter.

Hay Lin stepped back. And that was when her mom took a good, long look at Hay Lin's face—her *made-up* face. Frowning, she took Hay Lin's powdered cheeks in her hands.

"My goodness!" her mother cried. "Have you looked at yourself in a mirror? Who put this makeup on you? A deranged painter?"

Ooops, Taranee thought. I guess I did go a little heavy on the lipstick and eyeliner!

Hay Lin glanced over her shoulder at Taranee and shrugged. She turned back to her mom.

"I'll never wear makeup, ever again!" Hay Lin announced. With dramatic flair, she closed her eyes and covered her heart with her hand. "I swear!"

Hay Lin's mom scratched her head. "That's not necessary, but maybe you should just ask for some advice next time." She tapped her cheek with her finger as she surveyed the heavy powder, blush, and lipstick. "It wouldn't be very difficult to do a better job than this."

"Really?" Hay Lin asked.

"Really," her mom assured her. Then they both burst out laughing.

"Oh, Mom!" Hay Lin exclaimed throwing herself back into her mother's arms.

Taranee wanted to laugh with them, but she was too nervous. She'd already overheard her own mother's voice in the next room, demanding to know where her daughter was being held.

Uh-oh. Here it goes, Taranee thought. I only hope she'll be as understanding as Hay Lin's mom!

"Taranee!"

Taranee tensed. She watched her mother march into the room. The expression on Judge Cook's angular face was something between a scowl and a sneer. Beneath the dark line of her bangs, her brown eyes flashed with fury.

Whoa, Taranee thought, I don't think my mom's in the mood for jokes about makeup. With a deep breath, she rose from the bench. "Let me explain," she began, "I—"

But she didn't get another word out. Just as Captain Coletti had, her mother cut her off.

"An article for the school paper, was it?" she snapped.

Taranee didn't think it was possible to feel any more embarrassed than she already did. But hearing Uriah and Kurt snicker on the bench behind her caused her to flush.

These guys already laugh at me enough as it is, Taranee thought sadly. Now they have another excuse.

Once more, Taranee turned to her mother and tried to speak up. But her mom cut her off again. "I should've imagined *he* had something to do with this!" she exclaimed, gesturing toward Nigel. By then he'd slumped down on the bench beside Uriah and Kurt in a desperate attempt to become invisible.

Taranee glanced over her shoulder and met Nigel's gaze. He looked away.

Hanging her head, Taranee turned back to her mother, but she couldn't look her in the eye. Instead, she stared at the dirty, scuffed floor. She wasn't ashamed of Nigel. She was ashamed of her mother for jumping to conclusions like that.

She's acting like a cold, emotionless judge, Taranee thought. She's not acting like a warm, caring *mother* . . . at least not like Hay Lin's!

Taranee's mom stepped closer. She reached under Taranee's chin and gently lifted her daughter's head.

Taranee didn't resist. She looked at her mother, and, for a moment, hope rose in her heart. She thought of the tender scene she'd just witnessed between Hay Lin and her mom. She thought of how they'd embraced and talked and finally laughed. She waited for her mom to say something forgiving, as Hay Lin's mom had, pull her into a hug, and hold her close.

Instead, Taranee's mom said, "I'm ashamed of you." Then she raised her hand high, and . . .

Slap!

Taranee stood staring in shock at her mother. She could not believe it. Her mother had struck her, right across the cheek! The force of the slap stung, and tears welled up in her eyes. Behind her, she heard Uriah and Kurt erupt into peals of loud laughter.

But the slap wasn't what hurt the most. The shame hurt more.

My mother totally humiliated me, Taranee

said to herself. Right here, in front of Uriah and Kurt! In front of Hay Lin and her mother! Even in front of *Nigel*!

In seconds, Taranee's embarrassment melted down into devastating disappointment. Then something deep and powerful began to simmer and boil inside her. The fire Guardian felt her rage roar to life.

After trying so hard to be the perfect daughter, after getting straight As, studying night and day—not to mention saving the universe!—this is the thanks I get? she thought. No patience. No understanding. Just an ugly, harsh slap of humiliation.

That was it. "You shouldn't have done that," Taranee told her mom through gritted teeth. "Not in front of everyone."

Her mother couldn't see the flames rising up inside her. But Taranee could feel them, burning away every last bit of restraint within; threatening to engulf the room in burning heat.

"I'm through with you, Mom!" she shouted, her fists clenched, her eyes flashing.

In that moment, Taranee made a devastating decision. She had had enough of being Little Miss Perfect.

Soon, she thought, my mother will be extremely sorry for the way she's treated me. Soon she'll realize that she can't control me anymore!

NINE

"So, do you like it?" Will's father asked.

Will held the frog up by its skinny green arms and regarded the little guy's coy smile.

It's completely adorable! she thought. I love its big, buggy eyes and silly smile. And its beanbag insides make it fun to hug, too!

How did he remember I loved all things froggy? Will wondered. After so many years without writing or calling or seeing me, how did he know what the perfect gift would be?

Will smiled at the stuffed frog, then met her dad's gaze. He smiled back. "You were always crazy about frogs," he said. "Right?"

"It's really nice . . ." she told him, but

then hesitated. This is so weird, she thought. It's been so long since I called him—"D—Da . . ."

"Don't be afraid to say it," her father coaxed. "I *am* your dad, after all!"

Will laughed nervously. She was about to try calling him Dad again when her mother stepped between them.

"What do you say we stop this charade right now, Thomas?" she snapped. "Can't you see you're just embarrassing her? What do you want from her? Do you want it to instantly go back to the way it was?"

Will shrank back as her mother pointed a finger at her dad's chest.

"Even if she doesn't remember everything, she knows perfectly well that you made our lives impossible for years!" her mom cried. "Or have you forgotten about your mysterious disappearances?"

The sharp tone of her mother's voice made Will cringe inside. Without thinking, she hugged her new froggy close. For a fleeting moment, she felt like a little girl again, lying in bed, listening wide-eyed to her parents' angry voices.

"And have you forgotten about our bank

accounts being cleaned out?" Will's mother went on. "And the arguments? Have you forgotten about your threats and your anonymous phone calls? We left Fadden Hills to get *away* from you, Thomas!"

A sad shadow fell over her father's face, and Will wondered if he really was sincere. He slowly shook his head. "I've changed, Susan."

"You haven't changed one bit!" Will's mom shot back. "If you'd become a reasonable person, you would've signed our divorce papers!"

Will gagged. *Divorce papers?* she repeated to herself.

"This morning, when my lawyer told me he hadn't gotten your signature, I knew you were up to something," her mom said, "but I never imagined this!"

Will couldn't believe what she was hearing. Her parents had been separated for years. She had assumed they were already divorced. Obviously, they weren't. Her mother was still legally married to her father!

No wonder Mom's so upset, Will thought. There's no way she can marry Mr. Collins—or anyone else—unless my dad signs those papers.

"I don't want to lose you," Will's father firmly told his wife. "And I don't want to lose Will, either! I love her!"

Whoa, whoa, whoa, Will thought. He loves me? He doesn't want to lose me? Where is this coming from after all this time? Why is he saying all of this now?

Will's mother put her hands on her hips. "You only love yourself, Thomas. And I don't want my daughter to suffer because of you anymore."

"I know I made a lot of mistakes," her father replied. "I wasn't the perfect husband, or the perfect father . . . but now I want to make up for lost time."

Will's mom shook her head and turned away.

"Give me another chance, Susan," her dad pleaded.

Will's mom folded her arms tightly and stood with her back to her husband.

Will rubbed her forehead in puzzlement. Mom's furious, she thought, but Dad seems like he really means it. What if he really has changed, like he says he has?

Just then, Will's dad turned to face her. "I

brought you something else, Will," he said, dipping his hand into his pants pocket. He pulled out a key chain with a little frog on it, and something else. "Here."

Will reached for the gift. "It's a key," she murmured.

Her dad smiled and nodded. He put an arm around her shoulders and led her to one of the living-room windows.

"It's the key to your surprise," he explained. "If you look out the window, you'll see it right down there, waiting for you."

Will peered through the window and gasped. She couldn't believe her eyes. Her father wasn't kidding!

"Wow! A motor scooter!" Will cried.

It was brand-new and bright red—the same shade of red as Will's hair!

"I can't believe it! It's fantastic! And . . . it's even got wheels," she joked.

Will's dad laughed. "And if you start it up, it actually *moves*, too!"

What do you know? Will thought with a giggle. My dad and I have the same color hair and the same sense of humor.

"Why don't you go try it out?" her dad

suggested, gesturing toward the door.

"For sure!" Will snatched up her jacket and began to bolt.

Unfortunately, she didn't get very far. Her mother blocked her exit. "Don't go near that door, Will!" she warned. "And I mean it!"

"But . . . but that's not fair!" Will cried. "Can't we even talk it over?"

"Not now!" her mom practically shouted. Then she closed her eyes, took a breath, and lowered her voice. "Go to your room, please." She pointed the way, as if Will needed directions.

Will stomped off, twisting her face into an exaggerated pout, just to make sure her mom knew she was *not* happy!

She's treating me like I'm still five! Will silently raged. But Dad gave *me* the gift! And he's still my dad! She shouldn't be able to stop him from giving me a present!

"Good night, sweetheart," Will's father called after her. "And don't worry! I'll try to make this hothead change her mind!"

As Will continued down the hall, she could still hear her parents' raised voices.

"I'm sorry, Susan," her father said. "I know

I acted on impulse. I should've talked with you about the scooter first."

"Do you even realize what you're doing, Thomas?" Will's mother replied. "After everything that's happened between us, you come back and expect to be welcomed with open arms?"

"I want to make up for the harm I've done," he said. "That's why I didn't sign those papers."

Will reached her bedroom door. She nervously glanced back toward the living room. Her mom was looking in her direction, as if waiting for her to vanish into her bedroom, so Will went inside and shut the door, but then immediately put her ear to it in order to continue eavesdropping.

"Listen, Thomas," Will heard her mother saying. "I don't—"

Will's dad interrupted her. "Don't say anything right now. Take all the time you need. Think it over, and . . . in the meantime, I hope you don't have any objections if I come to see Will once in a while."

"I can't stop you from doing that, and you know it," Will's mom said.

"She and I have a lot of things to tell each

other," her father replied, "and we have a lot of lost time to make up for."

"You watch your step, Thomas," Will's mom warned. "Will's an intelligent girl, and you won't be able to buy her trust with gifts!"

"That was just a way to say I'm sorry," her dad admitted. "A pretty lousy way, I admit, but a way nonetheless."

Will's parents kept talking, but their voices became muffled. She could tell they were moving across the living room and toward the front door. Finally, she heard her father say, "Bye, Susan."

Then the front door closed, and the apartment became as silent as a grave. Will considered leaving her room to talk to her mom. She reached for the doorknob, but her hand froze.

What would I say? Will wondered. I don't even know how I feel!

Like the multicolored flashes of their Guardian energies, an array of emotions swirled around inside of Will. Anger, fear, confusion, excitement, and hope tangled together in a confusing ball.

Is my dad really back to stay? Will asked herself. Is there any chance Mom will forgive him so that they can stay together?

Will collapsed onto her bed and hugged her new froggy toy.

What will happen now? she wondered. Is my dad going to move into our apartment? Or will he want us to move into his place? Where does he live now anyway? Does he own a town house in the historic district? Or maybe he's renting a supercool penthouse apartment like the one Cornelia's family lives in.

Will thought of Cornelia—and Hay Lin, Taranee, and Irma, too. All of the other Guardians had families with mothers and fathers.

Maybe I'm finally on my way to living that way again, too, Will thought. Then she let out a big yawn.

Closing her eyes, she tightened her arms around her toy frog. As she drifted off to sleep, she tried to imagine what her life would be like if her parents got back together . . . and were happy.

Will looked around in confusion. It was the middle of the night, and she was no longer in bed. She stood at one end of a wide hallway.

Statues lined the edges, and a long red carpet led to a pair of elegant white doors.

Will approached the doors which opened smoothly, as if by magic. Inside, an immense ballroom was crowded with people. Will admired the high, arched ceiling and tall French windows. Outside, the night was dark; but inside, the chandeliers gave the room a golden glow.

Decorative purple bunting had been draped all around the room. Numerous buffet tables were covered in white linen and loaded with delicious appetizers and silver punch bowls.

As Will moved into the ballroom, she became aware that she was not properly dressed. Her jeans and long-sleeved T-shirt didn't look right at all. The people around her were dressed in elegant silks and satins.

She took another look at the people around her. *Wait!* she thought. There's something weird about their clothes. They're old, *really* old, like, from the seventeenth century old!

The women's gowns looked like the kind Will had seen in history books about France. The men's suits involved short breeches, knee-high stockings, waistcoats, and capes!

And what's with their hair? Will wondered.

She peered at the revelers realizing that most of them were wearing wigs—white, powdered wigs. And everyone was holding carved wooden masks over their faces!

Omigosh, Will thought, this is a costume ball! But what am I doing here? I don't have a costume!

"Hello, there!" called a man and woman, walking up to her.

The young couple looked even more elegant than the rest of the crowd. The woman wore an ice-blue gown that contrasted beautifully with her sleek black hair. The man wore a bright red waistcoat and a swashbuckling Musketeer hat with a plume. Their faces were hidden behind masks.

Will felt flustered and embarrassed by her own grungy appearance. "I'm sorry!" she told them quickly. "But I can't find my costume!"

"How dreadful," said the young woman. Then she and her escort removed their masks.

Will gasped. The young woman was Mandy Anderson! And her date was Matt Olsen!

"Why don't you conjure up a costume with your magic?" Mandy asked Will with a sneer.

Matt narrowed his eyes. "That is, if you can," he added mockingly.

"No-o-o-o-o!" Will cried.

They laughed at her, and she turned and ran blindly into the crowd. A tall, elegant woman suddenly moved in front of her, blocking her way.

The woman removed her blank-featured mask, and Will's eyes widened. "Mom?"

"I told you not to come here!" Will's mother cried.

Beside her mom stood a tall man with broad shoulders. He held a mask to his face, too. But unlike the others, his wasn't blank. Will immediately recognized the face.

"Dad!" she exclaimed. "At least you—"

"Trust me, Will," her father said, cutting her off. "Trust me."

Will nodded, and he finally removed the mask that had been sculptured to resemble his eyes, nose, and mouth. What he revealed underneath, however, wasn't a normal face. It was a white, featureless skull!

"*Aaagh!*"

Will screamed herself awake and then sat straight up in bed. Her heart was beating fast, and her hands were clammy with sweat.

She looked around. Peering. among the shadows of her dark bedroom, she reassured herself that she was home and that she was safe. She was no longer at some demented costume ball.

With a sigh, she realized that what she'd experienced hadn't been real at all.

It was only a dream, she thought. It didn't mean anything!

Then she hugged her stuffed froggy, snuggled back beneath her covers, and tried to blot out the nightmare and its terrible final image . . . to forget that when her father had removed his mask, there'd been nothing underneath but a skull.

TEN

When the final bell rang, Irma walked down Sheffield Institute's main hall, taking inventory. Still on the hunt for a crush, she appraised each boy she passed like a savvy shopper.

There were tall boys and short ones. There were skinny boys and tubby ones. Some had reasonably bright looks on their faces. Others appeared lost in another dimension.

If only I could tell them about the dimensions I've been to! she joked to herself.

She continued to survey the boys as they grabbed coats out of their lockers and packed books into their backpacks and messenger bags. Unfortunately, not a single one of these male specimens made her heart thump any faster than normal.

Why is this so hard? she wondered, scratching her head and tugging on her shoulder-length brown hair. A girl should be able to order up the perfect boy . . . as if she were ordering a pizza!

Irma blinked as she considered the idea. *Wow,* she thought, *what a great service that would be!*

"I'd like him tall, but not too tall," she murmured as she continued down the hallway. "Blond would be nice. Smart but not nerd level. Blue eyes like mine and his own motor scooter—but hold the anchovies."

"Irma? What are you doing?" Cornelia asked, breaking into Irma's thoughts. The blond-haired girl came striding up to her.

"Boy-hunting, what do you think?" Irma shrugged. "You and Caleb may have broken up, and Will may have given up on Matt. But Hay Lin and Taranee are already *double-dating* with Eric and Nigel, and I want a piece of that action!"

Cornelia rolled her eyes. She and Irma rarely saw eye to eye, and Irma knew that Corny was probably doing her best not to snap at her. After all, Irma had just brought up the never-to-be-mentioned ex. "Come on," she said, tugging Irma's coat sleeve and ignoring the remark. "Let's find Will. I'm worried about her."

The girls joined the swarm of kids exiting the building. The air felt chilly, but the sky was clear, and the afternoon sun was gorgeously bright. Irma squinted as she and Cornelia strolled out of Sheffield's front doors and into the grassy courtyard.

"There they are," Irma said. She pointed out Taranee and Hay Lin. They were talking with Will near one of the old oak trees.

When they reached their fellow Guardians, however, Irma quickly realized that Taranee and Hay Lin were the ones doing all the talking. Will was hanging her head. She looked really down and distracted.

Cornelia and Irma said hello, and the girls chatted for a moment. Then, together, the five friends headed for the front gate.

"Will's been totally bummed for a while now," Cornelia whispered to Irma as they walked along the concrete path. "She's been acting so strange."

"Well, at least she's not acting as strange as Taranee," Irma quietly confided. "Today she turned in a totally blank quiz sheet."

"Well . . ." Cornelia flipped back her long blond hair. "Don't you think it can happen to her, too, not to know any of the answers?"

"But that's what's so strange about it!" Irma said. "She knew the answers! She knew all of them. She whispered them all to me, but she didn't write any of them down."

"I can hear you, you know!" Taranee called over her shoulder.

"Oops!" Irma clapped a hand over her mouth.

Cornelia shot her a dirty look.

You don't have to say it, Irma thought as she looked over at her friends. You want the water girl to stop running her mouth!

Cornelia turned to Taranee. "Is it true, what Irma said?"

Taranee shrugged. "Completely true."

Hay Lin furrowed her brow. "But if you knew the answers, why did you do that?"

Taranee pushed her round glasses up on her nose. "I've decided to teach my mother a lesson. I always respected the rules of the house, and I always did well in school. But at the station she said she was *ashamed* of me."

Taranee looked down and shook her head. "I saw how your mom treated you, Hay Lin," she went on quietly. "Sure, she was upset. But mine *slapped* me in front of everybody without even listening to what I had to say." She shook her fist. "Well, now she's going to find out what it's like to have a daughter she really should be ashamed of!"

A flock of gulls suddenly took off from the high roof of the school. For a moment, their cawing and the flapping of their wings were deafening. Irma followed the birds with her eyes, then looked back at Taranee. She had never seen her friend so crushed and angry at the same time. She didn't know what to say to her.

"You're scaring me," Hay Lin finally said to Taranee. "You've never talked like this before."

Irma quickly nodded in agreement. "You can't be serious."

"I am," Taranee assured them.

"But . . ." Irma chewed her lip, trying to think of a way to change Taranee's mind. "If you stop studying, *who's* going to let me copy her homework?"

Irma put a hand to her head in a theatrical

swoon and waited for the girls to laugh. They didn't. All she got was dead silence.

Oh, come on! she thought. That was funny!

"You better think it over, Taranee," Cornelia warned her. "If you do this, you'll be risking your grades and your whole life."

"I don't care," Taranee replied.

"You like doing well in school," Cornelia insisted. "Don't ruin everything just to get back at your mom."

"Cornelia's right!"

Everyone stared in surprise. Will had just spoken. She'd been silent and distracted up till then. But Irma was glad to see that their leader finally tuned in!

"Teaming up, are you?" Taranee said, but she didn't say it in anger. There was a little smile on her face, as if she knew her friends were just trying to look out for her.

The Guardians exchanged uncertain looks.

"Whatever . . ." Taranee shrugged. "For now, this is just what I feel like doing."

The Guardians followed Taranee as she walked out onto the sidewalk, toward the bus stop.

"Hey, Will!" a girl's voice called.

Irma turned to see a tall girl with long dark hair rushing up to them. Who's she? Irma wondered. Whoever she was, she didn't go to Sheffield. Irma would have remembered a girl as pretty and as perky as that one.

Just then, Will groaned.

Before Irma could ask Will what was wrong, the dark-haired girl was among them. "Great news, Will!" she exclaimed.

Will rolled her eyes and shot her friends a look that said, *Just what I needed!*

"I've got great news!" the girl repeated, catching her breath.

"Hi, Mandy," Will murmured dully.

"There's been a change," the girl explained. "Mr. Deplersun looked over the times of all the tryouts . . . and I was the best of the ones who didn't qualify! They're letting me into the meet, too!"

Irma didn't know who this Mandy was, but she did seem pretty happy about her news. The only thing Irma didn't get was why Will looked so *un*happy about it.

"Where are you going to practice?" Will asked in the same flat tone of voice.

"At your pool! That's why I'm here. I asked

the coach, and he said it was okay." Mandy grinned. "We'll be training together every day!"

Irma noticed Matt Olsen walking down the sidewalk toward the group. He clearly saw them, and she was about to wave. For some strange reason, however, he quickly looked the other way and crossed the street.

Irma wondered what he was hiding from. She scratched her head as she went back to considering this girl she didn't know. "Mandy . . . Mandy . . ." she mumbled. "Why does that name ring a bell?"

Will's frown deepened and she shoved her hands into her pockets. But she didn't explain.

"Of course!" Irma shouted, suddenly remembering. "It's from that song by Cobalt Blue!"

Mandy laughed as Irma pretended to be Matt, the band's lead singer. She put a fist to her mouth as if she were holding a microphone. Then she began to sing. *"Mandy, sweet as candy, you're my first love, and you send me above—"*

"Okay, I admit it!" Mandy cried with a grin. "That Mandy was me."

"Wow! That is totally cool!" Irma replied,

but her bubbly attitude was suddenly deflated by a sharp jab to her ribs.

YOW! Irma thought. That did *not* tickle!

She turned to Hay Lin, whose skinny elbow had done the jabbing. "What's wrong with you?" Irma demanded angrily.

Hay Lin's fake grin revealed her W.I.T.C.H. braces. "Use your brain once in a while," she advised.

Huh? Irma thought. Did I miss something? But before she had a chance to question Hay Lin again, she heard a loud noise.

SCREEEK!

The girls looked up to find a hot sports car pulling up to the curb next to them. Irma's blue eyes widened at the sight of the expensive convertible. A broad-shouldered guy with red hair was at the wheel, but she couldn't see his face.

Still on the hunt for a potential boyfriend, Irma couldn't help asking, "Who's that driving the Super Spider?" Just then, the driver turned, and Irma got a good look at his face. *Ugh*, she thought. Totally too old!

"That's my father, Irma," Will announced.

"Your *father*?" Irma whispered, her eyes widening in shock. "Whaaaaa?"

Will didn't stick around to explain. Instead, she darted toward the shiny blue convertible. Her father smiled as she climbed into the front seat beside him.

Irma glanced at the girls around her. They looked as shocked as she felt—all except for Mandy, who looked sad, for some reason.

"I hope she realizes how lucky she is. . . ." Mandy whispered.

Irma didn't know what Mandy was talking about, but she didn't care at the moment. The news about Will's father's being back in her life was a complete stunner.

"Do you guys know anything?" Hay Lin asked.

"Zero!" Taranee replied.

Cornelia shook her head. "Will never told us anything about him."

"It's a mystery," Irma mumbled.

Mr. Vandom revved the engine of his convertible and sped down the street, leaving the four worried friends in the exhaust.

ELEVEN

"The last thing I want is to leave Heatherfield like I had to leave Fadden Hills," Will's father explained. "After all, now that you've shown me where to get the best burger in town, how *could* I leave?"

Will laughed. "You're right!"

She was sitting across the table from her father in a cozy, cushioned booth. He had let Will choose the restaurant for dinner, and it hadn't been a hard choice.

What with her mom being in a bad mood at home, and Irma singing that stupid Cobalt Blue song about Mandy, Will had needed to smother her sorrows. Her remedy was a triple cheeseburger and a big side of fries, and that prescription could be filled in only one place—the Golden Diner.

"I'm happy your mom gave you permission to see me," Will's dad told her.

Will finished chewing a big, greasy bite of cheeseburger. "Me, too," she said, wiping her mouth with a napkin.

For days her parents had fought on the phone about it. Finally, her mother had given in and allowed her father to take Will out, and Will was glad. She would have been eating alone that night anyway.

At that very moment, her mom was out on a date with Mr. Collins. He had made reservations at a fancy restaurant on the other side of town. Will wasn't surprised that he was going to so much trouble. Her teacher was probably feeling the heat of competition, with her dad back in town. He must have figured that a nice dinner out would impress her mom and at least make her feel better.

It wouldn't impress me, though, Will thought. I'm glad I chose the Golden Diner for dinner with my dad. It feels so comfortable and familiar . . . like home.

"Even though I just found you again," her dad said, "I can already tell you're special. Not that that is a surprise. You always were . . ."

Her dad smiled and gazed off, as if into the past. Then he began to talk about a time when they'd all lived together in Fadden Hills.

Will had been very little, no more than two. She'd held her father's hand as they walked along the sidewalk one evening.

Her dad even remembered what she'd been wearing: a cute little blue jumper and red-and-white striped shirt.

"What's that, Daddy?" a little Will had squealed, pointing to a bright white globe in the night sky.

"That's the moon, honey," Will's dad had replied. "Do you like it?"

"No!" Will had cried, tugging hard on his pant leg. "Turn it off!"

Will loved hearing her dad's story.

"Turn off the moon!" she repeated, laughing hysterically. She pounded the table so hard her fries jumped into the air. "I don't remember that at all!" she cried.

"But it's true," he insisted. "You can even ask your mom. You had a knack for exploring things, down to the smallest detail."

"What do you mean?" Will asked.

"Well . . ." Her father scratched his head for a moment. "Do you remember that pink stuffed animal? The big slug?"

Will nodded. "Of course! His name was Pingeero!" The slug had been one of her favorites. He had had a funny antenna and plump ridges on his back.

Now that I think about it, Will realized, draining her big glass of soda, good old Ping would have felt right at home with the creatures of Metamoor!

"And do you remember the cruel fate you had him meet?" her dad asked.

Will had been crunching the ice in her drink. She suddenly froze in midcrunch. "No-o-o-o!" she wailed. "Why'd you remind me!"

Will now remembered what had happened to her stuffed slug. She'd been curious about his insides, so one night she'd ripped him open and pulled out all his stuffing.

Now I know what my dad meant about my habit of exploring things down to the smallest detail! Will thought. Poor little Pingeero.

Her dad laughed. "Oh, don't worry!" he said, waving his hand. "You did even worse things."

Will's eyebrows rose. She was almost scared to hear more, but she was having too much fun! She just had to ask. . . . "Like *what*?"

Will's dad told her about the day of her kindergarten play. . . .

Will's father and mother had looked for her in the backyard, but she hadn't been there. Then they'd checked the living room and her bedroom. No Will. She had seemed to be missing.

"Will?" her mom had called through the house. "Where are you?"

"You don't want to be late for your play, do you?" her dad called out.

A moment later, her mother had started crying, "No-o-o-o-o!"

Will had carried her little stool into her parents' room. She'd climbed atop it and gotten hold of the brush, comb, and scissors on her mom's dresser, and she'd used every single one of them on her hair, especially the scissors!

"What do you mean, 'especially the scissors'?" Will asked her dad.

"You took a big handful of your hair and cut it completely off," he explained. "You had this two-inch patch of bare scalp. You looked ridiculous."

Will gasped. "What did you and Mom do?"

Her dad smiled. "Your mom found a cute hat with a frog on it. And she made you wear it every day until your hair grew back in."

"*Omigosh!*" Will was practically crying with laughter. "I think I actually remember that hat!"

Will and her dad continued to laugh as they finished their meal. Her dad paid the check, and then they headed out. His convertible was parked nearby, and they strolled toward it.

"Those were the days," Will said after her dad finished telling another funny story.

"Everything will be like that again now, I promise," he said, as he unlocked the passenger door. "And . . . seeing as your new scooter's been *banned by the powers that be*, I'll drop you off at the pool."

Will giggled. "If Mom heard you talk like that . . ."

"You're not going to tell her, are you?" her dad teased.

Will shook her head and climbed into her dad's cool car. He got behind the wheel and started the engine.

Will realized she loved driving around in the car with her dad. The engine purred smoothly as the car sped along. With the top down, she could feel the breeze lifting her bright red hair into the air. She felt free . . . and happy.

As they raced down the street, Will rose up so she could look out above the windshield. The breeze felt much stronger above the glass.

"Can I?" she asked her dad, as she tucked her legs under her and rose higher in the seat.

He smiled. "Of course!"

VROOM! VROOM!

Her dad revved the engine and put the pedal to the metal. As they flew through the city, Will extended her arms out as if she were really flying.

This is incredible! she thought as the wind whooshed through her hair.

She glanced at her dad. He was smiling as

he drove, clearly pleased that she was having a good time.

Will *was* having a good time. She couldn't believe how much fun their dinner had been. She was also surprised at her dad's vivid memories of Fadden Hills and what she had been like as a little girl. Her own memories of her father were fuzzy at best. Most of what she remembered was his fighting with her mom, her mom crying bitterly, and then her dad's simply being gone.

Will wondered what her best friends had thought earlier, seeing her get into her dad's car after school. She'd never told them much about him because she simply hadn't known much. It had been easier to stay quiet than bring up sad memories of the past.

Plus, Will didn't want anyone's pity. And she didn't want to be asked questions she couldn't answer. So she'd never brought up the subject of her father, and her friends had never asked.

Now, however, Will figured they'd want to know everything. Well, this dinner was a start, she decided. She would tell her friends all about it.

Even if her mom didn't stay married to her dad, Will didn't see why she couldn't see her father. They could have dinners like this all the time!

Maybe I really did get my father back, Will thought. Maybe everything will turn out okay. Sure, he's not the way I remember him. But, I still like him!

TWELVE

A few days later, Cornelia was sitting with Irma, sipping hot cocoa at the Pumpkin Café.

Mmmm . . . yum, she thought. The Golden Diner has the best milk shakes in Heatherfield, but nobody can touch the Pumpkin's cocoa!

The café's chocolate was really high-quality. Plus, as an added bonus, they topped each order with one's choice of whipped cream or homemade marshmallows. Cornelia always went for the marshmallows.

Not Irma. She ordered her cocoa with whipped cream. When a dollop of it ended up on the tip of her nose, Cornelia laughed.

"What?" Irma said. "Did I say something funny?"

Cornelia pulled a small mirror out

of her bag and held it up. Irma rolled her eyes and wiped the whipped cream off her nose. "You could have just *told* me," she griped.

The two had come there to discuss their friends, especially Will and Taranee. While Will's mood had improved over the past week, Taranee's had plummeted.

The fire Guardian had been sullen at school. And she absolutely refused to discuss going back on her decision to sabotage her own grades.

At lunch earlier that day, Taranee had told W.I.T.C.H. about the latest developments at home. Her mother had seen her homework grades for the week—straight Fs. She'd also seen her pop quiz grades, which were no better.

Instead of sitting down with Taranee and talking over what was really wrong, her mom had hit the ceiling. She had ranted and raved about grade point averages and college admissions, and then she had grounded Taranee.

Judge Cook had then marched her daughter into her home office and forced her to study in her paneled den. "In light of your recent failures," she'd said, "you'll be studying here from now on, so you'll have fewer distractions."

The leather-bound legal volumes on the shelves were supposed to inspire Taranee to buckle down.

"I went along with being relocated to the monster's lair," she'd told her W.I.T.C.H. friends, "but there's no way I'm doing any homework while I'm in there."

"Then what *do* you do in there?" Cornelia had asked.

Taranee had shrugged. "Read her legal files, mostly."

Cornelia could sort of see what Taranee was trying to accomplish. By blowing off her schoolwork, she hoped to force her mom into dealing with her as a human being.

However, Cornelia was worried that it might take a long, long time for Judge Cook to figure that out—so long, in fact, that Taranee might just ruin her future first.

Taranee wasn't the only Guardian about whom Cornelia was concerned. There was also Will. Cornelia knew that Matt's betrayal had been a really harsh blow and that the whole deal with her dad showing up in Heatherfield had made Will's life even more complicated. Will had been keeping superbusy, training every evening for the citywide swim meet. All of that swimming was definitely helping to improve her mood, but the tension between her mom and dad was weighing on her.

Cornelia knew that Will was pretty happy about spending time with her dad. But she also knew that Will probably felt guilty about betraying her mom. It was probably always on Will's mind, Cornelia thought. You don't just adjust to something like a parent's reemergence that easily. Or, a boy's breaking your heart.

Automatically, Cornelia's fingers tightened around her cup of cocoa. *Boys*, she thought bitterly. They really knew how to let a girl down!

Cornelia still dreamed about the boy who had betrayed her. None of her friends knew that, because she seldom talked about Caleb anymore. Talking about him only made the pain worse.

On some days, Cornelia was really busy, or totally focused on her friends and family. Worrying about other people's troubles was one way she had found to make her own pain recede.

Other days, when she had the time to sit and think, the heartache came back worse than ever. She'd wonder what Caleb was doing on Metamoor. She'd wonder if he were happy or if he'd fallen in love again. She'd wonder if he were thinking about *her*.

"What do you say, Cornelia?" Irma whispered across their café table. "What if I fall in love with *him*?"

Cornelia blinked to clear her head of Caleb. "What did you say?" she asked.

"Him," Irma repeated, jerking her thumb in the direction of a guy standing at the café counter. "What do you think?"

Cornelia quickly realized that Irma was back to her boy-hunting ways again. She glanced at the boy Irma was interested in. He was tall, but not as tall as Caleb, Cornelia noted. He had an average build—but again, not as nice as Caleb's.

Cornelia couldn't see the boy's face, because he was turning away from them. She could see his hair, though. It was a lighter shade of brown than Caleb's, and much longer, falling way past his shoulders.

Cornelia shrugged. Any boy who wasn't Caleb really didn't impress her. "If you're into that kind of guy, I guess he's okay," she said.

While Cornelia quietly sipped her cocoa, Irma batted her eyelashes flirtatiously. "Hey, you!" she called.

The guy turned around and smiled at Irma. "You talking to me?"

Cornelia nearly choked on her cocoa.

The guy's crooked teeth, smashed-in nose, and bloodshot eyes made him a prime candidate for Hollywood's next scary movie.

Clearly trying not to gag, Irma quickly told the guy she'd made a mistake. "Uh, thought you were somebody else," she said. "Never mind!"

Cornelia had to bite her tongue to keep from laughing.

But then she checked herself. All of Irma's boy-hunting made her wonder—would she be ready for a boyfriend ever again.

Maybe *after* Irma finds one, I can try, Cornelia decided. But, knowing Irma, that probably means I have some time!

THIRTEEN

Will bounded happily down the sidewalk toward her apartment building. Her red hair smelled of the chlorinated pool, and her limbs were slightly sore from the afternoon's swim practice.

Coach Deplersun's about as easygoing as a drill sergeant, she thought. But he's gotten me into the best shape of my life!

The citywide swim meet was only a few days away; Will couldn't wait to get to her numbered block and hear that starting gun go off. Her lane of blue water would stretch out before her, and she'd race to the winning position! She was sure of it!

The only thing that brought her down these days was thinking about

Matt. Will hated to admit it, but . . . she missed him.

She and Matt had used to talk about everything. If they didn't see each other at school, they'd talk afterward, at his grandfather's pet shop. They had chatted on their phones at night, e-mailed each other on weekends, and sent text messages to each other between classes.

Before Mandy had come along, they'd been really close. Will missed that.

"And whom do I blame for losing my best friend as well as my boyfriend?" she muttered. "Mandy!" Will sighed in disgust. "Mandy, Mandy, Mandy . . . She's sweet, funny, pretty, and nice, and I can't stand her!"

It's no wonder I've resorted to tricks, she thought.

In fact, Will's latest trick had been her best so far. She'd used it at swim practice earlier. . . .

The coach had been clocking the girls, one at a time. Will had gone first. She'd nailed her best time yet for the freestyle swim, and the coach had praised her effort.

Two more girls took their turns. He corrected some of their faults. Finally, it was

Mandy's turn to get in the pool and show her freestyle stuff.

When she began to swim, however, something mysterious cramped her style.

"Oh, come on!" the coach yelled at Mandy. "Now you can't even do the dog paddle!"

"It's not my fault!" Mandy wailed. "It's as if my legs are made of lead! It's incredible!"

Hanging out at the side of the pool, Will chuckled to herself. It's not incredible, she thought. It's magic!

She'd used her internal energies to throw Mandy way off her best game. And she didn't feel guilty in the least.

Oh, sure, a part of Will knew that what she was doing wasn't very nice, but she felt more than justified, just the same. After all, Mandy had taken Will's boyfriend away. And Mandy had gotten a song written about her.

Well, Will thought, Mandy isn't going to get everything!

As Will walked through the front door of her building, she laughed to herself.

Mandy doesn't know how lucky she is! Will thought. Up to now, I've been *easy* on her!

After all, Will and her friends were plenty powerful. W.I.T.C.H. had saved Metamoor *and* destroyed Nerissa. Mandy was nothing in comparison.

The Oracle wouldn't have approved of what Will was doing. She knew that. In the scheme of things, however, Will believed she'd earned the right to use a trick or two.

Will stepped out of the elevator and headed down the hall. As she moved closer to her apartment, she heard voices coming from inside. One of them, for sure, was her mother's. The other voice was a man's.

Will carefully turned the knob of her front door. She quietly opened and cocked an ear to hear better.

"I got a hotel room here in town," she heard a deep voice say. "I want to be close to Will . . . and to you."

Will recognized her father's voice. He was speaking with her mom.

She carefully pushed the door open a little more and crouched down so she could peek in. Will's mother was mumbling something so low that Will couldn't hear it. Then Mr. Vandom spoke again.

"What do you say to this?" he asked.

Will peered inside and stifled a gasp. *This* turned out to be a ring! Was Will's dad presenting her mom with a wedding ring?

For a moment, Will was totally psyched. This is it! she thought. They're going to get back together!

Unfortunately, her prediction was way off.

"Here's what I have to say to that!" her mom exclaimed.

Smack! She slapped the ring away.

"Susan," Will's dad responded. "I just want my family back."

"Take it or leave it, huh?" her mother snapped. "That's a game you've played your whole life, but your routine won't work on us anymore!"

"Be careful what you say, Susan," her father warned.

Will sighed. Here we go again, she thought in despair.

"You know . . ." her father said slowly, "you shouldn't provoke me."

"Don't you dare threaten me!" Will's mom shouted. "Try hurting me or Will, and I'll make you pay for it!"

"We'll see, Susan," her father said. "We'll see who'll pay."

Will sighed. She was sad to see her mom rejecting her dad so harshly. She knew her mom could be stubborn; she was clearly still angry about Will's dad's messing up in the past. But Will held on to the thought that she'd change her mind.

I hope my dad won't stop trying to work things out, Will found herself thinking. He should just hold on to that ring. Eventually, Mom's sure to come around!

A few days later, Will arrived at the city pool for the big swim meet. Unfortunately, Mandy arrived at the same time, and the two entered the building together.

"Hey, Mandy . . ." Matt called out from the stands.

Will froze. Hearing his voice still made her heart beat faster and her hands go clammy.

"Look," Mandy said, touching Will's arm. "Matt's here."

"Uh-huh," Will mumbled, refusing to look his way.

"Go for it, Will!" a man called out from the

stands. "You can do it!"

"Hey," said Mandy, "isn't that—"

"Yeah!" Will said, her spirits lifting. "It's my dad!" She turned and waved, grinning when she saw his thumbs-up sign. "I guess it's a little embarrassing, but . . ."

Mandy shook her head. "It's not embarrassing. It's sweet," she told Will. "He's here just for you."

Will knew Mandy was right. No matter what her mother thought of her dad, he was there to support her. And for now, that was what mattered most.

HEY, MANDY!

OH, LOOK . . . MATT'S HERE.

UH-HUH.

GOOD LUCK, WILL! YOU CAN DO IT!

IS THAT YOUR DAD?

YEAH. HE'S A LITTLE OVER THE TOP . . . ALMOST EMBARRASSING. BUT . . .

IT'S NOT EMBARRASSING AT ALL! IT'S SWEET. HE'S HERE FOR YOU . . .

WILL, CAN YOU TELL THE COACH I'M PULLING OUT? I'VE BEEN SUCH A DISASTER LATELY, ANYWAY . . .

UH-UH. I'M NOT TELLING HIM ANYTHING. IF THAT'S YOUR DECISION, YOU TELL HIM.

I HAVEN'T BEEN ABLE TO ENJOY SWIMMING SINCE IT STARTED. DID THAT HAPPEN TO YOU, TOO?

?

UGH... WHAT'VE I DONE? I'VE BEEN HORRIBLE TO MANDY!

UM... WELL... NOT REALLY. BUT I DID LOSE A LOT OF MY FRIENDS...

THAT HAPPENED TO ME, TOO! ALL OF THEM EXCEPT MATT...

THE NIGHT MY PARENTS TOLD ME THE BAD NEWS, I CALLED HIM, AND HE WAS SO SWEET TO ME...

OH... SO SHE WAS THE GIRL MATT WAS HUGGING.

THANKS TO MY ASTRAL DROP, I'VE RUINED EVERYTHING. I HAVE TO MAKE IT RIGHT!

WHICH WAY IS IT?

THIS WAY!

SLAM

OUCH!

NICE GOING, EINSTEIN! ARE YOU SURE YOU'VE BEEN HERE BEFORE?

OVER THERE! I CAN HEAR PEOPLE CLAPPING.

OH, NO! WE'RE TOO LATE.

FIRST PLACE: MANDY ANDERSON!

THANKS FOR CONVINCING ME TO RACE TODAY, WILL.

LET'S JUST SAY I OWED YOU ONE. BESIDES, I MIGHT'VE LOST THE RACE, BUT I WON A NEW FRIEND.